Lovingly Yours, Lydia

THE DIARY AND CORRESPONDENCE OF THE YOUNGEST BENNET SISTER

FRED SCHLOEMER

BUTLER BOOKS

Cover design by Scott Stortz

ISBN 978-1-941953-58-7

Printed in the United States of America

Published by
Butler Books
P.O. Box 7311
Louisville, KY 40257
phone: (502) 897-9393
fax: (502) 897-9797
www.butlerbooks.com

To my husband and best friend, Ernie Schnell,
for his constant love, patience, and support while
reading multiple iterations of this book.

And to my favorite author, Jane Austen, with
true awe and reverence for her genius.

Contents

Preface

JANE AUSTEN'S *Pride and Prejudice*, A COMEDY OF MANNERS
with some very serious themes about Georgian-era English
gentry, is one of the most beloved works in literature. Part of its
enduring charm is the grace and wit with which Austen charac-
terizes people who, while products of a special time in history,
are recognizable today. Not the least of these is the feckless
Lydia, youngest of the Bennet sisters, and source of many of the
story's tensions.

It is easy to disdain Lydia for her self-absorption—until we
remember that she was merely a child, and thus, hardly can be
blamed for her lack of depth. By today's standards especially,
when adult children often live with their parents well into their
twenties and even thirties, perhaps Lydia deserves more compas-
sionate consideration. She is, in many ways, the quintessential
anti-heroine, whom her family loves in spite of herself.

One of my favorite exercises as a writer is to imagine the *other*
side of any story. I recently enjoyed P. D. James's sequel, *Death
Comes to Pemberley*, and admired the spin she put on Austen's
classic. Her treatment of the characters and story was thoroughly
engaging.

At the same time, I found myself wondering, "What must it
have been like to be Lydia? Was she aware of being considered
a silly, selfish girl, and if she was, would she have cared? As she

grew older, and, in all probability, began to suffer the effects of her dashing husband's narcissism, was there anyone she could turn to who really cared about her happiness and well-being?

I doubted it.

Given all that, I wondered, would she have become the long-suffering victim, whining about her lot to anyone who would listen? Or would she have struck out on her own, pursuing her destiny?

The first scenario is probable, as Lydia was a whiner of the highest order. The second is far less likely, as the culture and mores of the time forced most women into dependency on men.

However, what of yet another possibility? Might Lydia have experienced subsequent life events that challenged her to deepen her character? She was married to a soldier in the midst of the Napoleonic Wars. As such, she might have followed her husband through his wartime travels. Many military wives of her era did, despite the tremendous hardships and challenges it presented— and, though feckless, Lydia could also be a very determined young woman.

That is where I have chosen to take my own sequel to Austen's tale—imagining Lydia having to grow up—perhaps not easily or happily, but inevitably, becoming a true adult, by making her way through one of the most deadly and difficult periods in Europe's history.

—Fred Schloemer

Pride and Prejudice:
Synopsis and Commentary

Pride and Prejudice IS A LOVE STORY AND COMEDY ABOUT THE lives of the gentry in Georgian England. The story takes place from 1812 to 1813, and is set in Meryton, a fictitious village in Hertfordshire, England. It tells the tale of the Bennets, a well-born but poor family of five sisters, a foolish mother, and a droll, long-suffering father.

The oldest sister, Jane, is a kind, soft-spoken beauty. The second-born, Elizabeth or Lizzie, is lovely as well, though appreciated more for her intellect than her beauty. The middle sister, Mary, is bookish and socially awkward. The youngest sisters, Catherine or Kitty, and Lydia are fun loving, boisterous, and inclined to be man crazy, especially for the officers stationed at a nearby garrison.

As was English law at the time, the Bennets' estate, Longbourn, is entailed, meaning it can pass only to a male heir. On Mr. Bennet's death, their ancestral home would go to a male cousin, the Reverend Collins, a self-absorbed social climber. From there, the Bennet ladies' fate would be uncertain. They would essentially be homeless unless the Reverend Collins or some other male relative provided for them.

Worse yet, the Bennets' reduced circumstances prevent them

from providing dowries to attract well-to-do suitors for their girls. Nonetheless, Mrs. Bennet is determined to marry off all her daughters, and strives obsessively to find them promising matches. After all, such matchmaking was the chief job of mothers of girls at the time, to secure their daughters' futures by finding them wealthy husbands.

The story opens with the handsome and amiable gentleman, Mr. Bingley, renting a nearby estate and attending a ball in the village with his haughty sisters. There, Jane and Bingley are attracted to each other, but Lizzie is put off by Bingley's best friend, Mr. Darcy, whom she considers proud and arrogant. Conversely, Darcy considers the Bennet girls an ill-behaved lot, unsuitable for the attentions of his closest friend.

Lizzie's dislike for Darcy deepens when she meets the handsome officer, Wickham, who tells her Darcy cheated him out of an inheritance. He says the two of them were raised as brothers by Darcy's father, but Darcy expelled him from the house when his father died, leaving him nothing.

Matters grow worse when Bingley and Darcy leave to winter in London, and Lizzie learns that Darcy has dissuaded Bingley from courting Jane. Jane visits friends in London, hoping to connect with Bingley, but Darcy withholds the information from him that she is in town. Believing Bingley is avoiding her, Jane returns to Longbourn, heartbroken.

A sub-plot involves Lizzie's best friend, good-hearted but plain Charlotte. Like the Bennets, she too comes from a good family (her father is a knight), but one with little money. Charlotte's story underscores one of the book's main themes, women's forced dependency on men in those days, especially poor and disadvantaged women.

The pompous Reverend Collins visits the Bennets and presumptuously offers Lizzie his hand in marriage. She firmly refuses him, and he is both surprised and offended. He considers himself quite a catch because he has the patronage of the powerful Lady Catherine de Bourgh, Darcy's aunt. He subsequently settles for Charlotte, much to Lizzie's chagrin, who feels that Charlotte has sold out.

When Lizzie visits newlywed Charlotte's parsonage home, her friend reassures her that she is content. She reminds Lizzie that she did, after all, have no other prospects. To Lizzie's surprise, Darcy calls on her while she is visiting Charlotte. In an unexpected twist, he confesses his secret love for her and asks her to marry him, despite expressing his distaste for her family. She angrily refuses him, denouncing him for his judgmental nature and cruelty to Wickham. The two part on bad terms, presumably for good.

However, the next day, Darcy again surprises Lizzie at the parsonage, dropping in to leave her a letter explaining himself. In it, he relates that Wickham has lied to her. The estrangement between the two men occurred because Wickham tried to seduce Darcy's innocent younger sister, Georgiana, in an attempt to lay hands on her fortune. He also describes the huge gambling debts Wickham ran up, and that he, Darcy, settled for him. Lizzie's angry dislike for Darcy begins to soften.

Soon afterward, Lizzie accompanies older relatives, the Gardiners, on a trip to Derbyshire, where Darcy's estate, Pemberley, is located. Once there, the Gardiners want to tour the countryside and end up at Pemberley, where the housekeeper offers to give them a tour.

Lizzie is hesitant, but agrees when she learns Darcy is away.

She falls in love with the beautiful house and grounds, and is surprised to learn that the staff consider Darcy a kind and generous employer and a loving, devoted brother to Georgiana. When Darcy comes home unexpectedly, Lizzie hastens to depart, but he pursues her, expressing pleasure at having seen her again. Over the next few days, she sees more of Darcy, meets his shy sister, and dines at Pemberley. She returns home with burgeoning feelings of admiration and respect for Darcy.

Wickham's regiment leaves Longbourn and goes to a military installation near Brighton. The youngest girls and Mrs. Bennet are bereft that all the handsome soldiers have left. Lydia manages to wheedle permission from her father to visit Brighton with family friends, the Forsters, as chaperones.

Before long, the Bennets receive the unhappy news that Wickham has eloped with Lydia, a scandal sure to ruin not only her reputation, but the entire family's name. Mr. Bennet rushes to find her, but eventually returns empty-handed. The family struggles to contain the unfolding scandal, but gossip of it rapidly spreads nonetheless.

Weeks pass, and the family receives the welcome news that Lydia and Wickham have married, saving them all from scandal. The newlyweds visit Longbourn, where Lydia lords it over the other girls, gloating that she, the youngest, is the first of them to marry.

Bingley and Darcy return to Meryton and visit the Bennet ladies. Bingley resumes his courtship of Jane, and Lizzie learns that Darcy has now encouraged Bingley to court her.

In the tale's denouement, Lizzie learns that Darcy tracked down the runaways in London, and offered Wickham a large settlement to marry Lydia. Touched by his intervention on their behalf, she realizes how wrongly she has misjudged him. She also realizes she loves him and soon accepts his second offer of marriage. Both couples—Lizzie and Darcy, and Jane and Bingley—are soon betrothed, and Mrs. Bennet is ecstatic to have another two of her girls paired off. The story ends with the two sisters' weddings.

—

The above synopsis offers only the barest glimpse at a story so rich with warmth, wit, and humor that it has become iconic. The book is remarkable for its grasp of human nature (particularly human foibles) and important social justice issues which transcend time:

- the oppressive effects of patriarchy;
- the dehumanizing effects of classist social customs;
- the challenges of developing meaningful relationships in a culture that values wealth over character; and
- the redemption to be found through addressing one's faults.

The book's impact is even more remarkable when we consider that it was written by a young, unmarried woman with little to no formal education. Though she was largely self-taught, she was nonetheless well taught. Critics through the years have described Austen's plots and characters as complex, her prose as flowing, and her syntax as flawless.

Certainly, I admire these aspects of her work. However, as a career psychotherapist, I find her keen insights into the workings of the human mind far more admirable. Austen could well have stood her own ground in a philosophical showdown with Sigmund Freud, Carl Jung, and William James.

It is with that sense of appreciation—even awe—for Austen's accomplishments, that I offer this follow-up to her most celebrated novel, *Pride and Prejudice*. While it will never equal her work, I hope it will entertain in the same spirit.

Author's Note

A FEW DETAILS DESERVE CLARIFICATION BEFORE OUR STORY begins.

In her original tale, Austen normally referred to Elizabeth Bennet with her proper name, rather than the nickname, Lizzie, which she and her closest friends and family used. I have chosen here to use the nickname exclusively, because the format of this story is a combination of Lydia's diary entries, and an exchange of letters between Lydia, Lizzie, and other characters. In these contexts, Elizabeth and her friends and family would have used her nickname.

In addition, it is important to note that the climax of *Pride and Prejudice* is the point in the story where Darcy makes his first, thwarted proposal to Lizzie, and soon after rescues Lydia from scandal. My story opens with Lydia and Wickham hiding out in an inn in London, still unmarried.

And, there, our tale begins . . .

PART ONE

Dreams and Realities

Prologue

Miss Catherine Bennet
Longbourn
Meryton, England

Dear Kitty,

I've done "it," at last . . . the very thing you and I have whispered about and giggled about and feared—but also wanted—for years. I am now a full-grown woman, at last! Such a lot to tell . . .

I was able to elude my chaperones at the Brighton Beachside Inn by slipping out two nights ago. I had already sent a message to George at the Preston Barracks, where he is stationed. He, of course, messaged me back right away, saying that he urgently wanted to see me. He eluded his fellow officers, as well, and soon scooped me up in his arms on the street outside the hotel.

He brought me here to this establishment, which a friend of his operates, and we have been in bliss ever since. Admittedly, it is not as grand or elegant a place as I would have hoped to make the setting for my first . . . well . . . you know. However, it is clean and respectable, and George's friend is most discreet. He promises he'll not let on to anyone that we're here, no matter who enquires, or how much money they offer him.

George is incredibly romantic. On our first night here, he threw open the windows and pointed to the moon and stars.

"The moon shall be our minister and the stars your bridesmaids, little Moppet!"

Moppet is his nickname for me, because of my head of curls, though I wish he would find a more dignified one. All my life, people have used the word "little" to describe me—little scamp, little flirt—and always with a little smile of derision. I know that they're thinking I'll never amount to anything.

Mark my words, Sister. Someday I am going to be a grand, dignified lady. I'm going to be so grand and dignified that people will come and bow before me and call me "Madam" or even "Highness." No one will call me "little" anything, anymore. Just wait and see, Kitty. I promise you, I will be a great lady someday.

Although, for now, I most certainly am not. Quite the contrary, I am "living in sin" with the most handsome man ever born. I suppose that is the choice I have made . . . to sin in exchange for happiness.

After pledging our troth before the moon and stars, George swept me off my feet and into bed, and . . . well, modesty forbids saying more about what followed. Only know this . . . after a little initial discomfort, it is absolutely divine! And George assures me he has methods for making sure I don't come down in the family way. I'm not sure what those are, but he is so smart and resourceful, I feel confident he knows what he's doing.

George has arranged for one of his fellow officers to carry this secret message to you at Longbourn, where he hopes to get it into the hands of one of the servants there to convey it to you. Please let me know by return secret message when you've gotten it.

Please, under no *circumstances let Mama and Papa know my whereabouts.*

I am blissfully happy and have no wish to be "saved."

Lovingly yours,

Lydia

Chapter 1

September 5, 1812

Dear Diary,

What a perfectly useless wedding gift to find in today's mail from Mary. I could very well use a tea cozy or linens, but no, she sends me a diary.

Doesn't she know not everyone enjoys sticking their nose between the pages of a book, day in and day out? Her note waxed on about how "enriching" she has found it through the years to record her thoughts and feelings about various life events. What life events would *those* be? Nothing ever happens to the gloomy girl, because she always has her nose stuck in a book.

I suppose I should be more charitable to the poor spinster. It *was* a nice thought, after all—and, may prove a useful a tool for recording all the parties and balls (and handsome men) I am encountering here in London, while George awaits further orders. He somehow managed to find a passable townhouse in the Whitechapel district.

Following our whirlwind elopement, George surprised me one day by insisting that we marry right away, although we had been together happily several weeks without benefit of a formal ceremony. He is *so* passionate! I never know what to expect from him.

We found a chapel and a pastor who performed a short ceremony. Imagine my surprise when we turned to leave, and found Darcy and Mr. Gardiner sitting grim-faced in the front pew. Rising to greet us, Darcy leaned down to give me a peck on the cheek and reached out to shake George's hand.

"Then, it is done," he said to George.

For some reason, the simple comment infuriated George.

"Yes, by God, it is done, and may He damn you for your interfering ways! The girl had no need of this farce. She was perfectly happy as we were."

Darcy seemed to force a tight smile and bade us good day. "May you live happily ever after," he called over his shoulder, as he and Mr. Gardiner left.

I was nonplussed. "Whatever was *that* about, George?"

He forced a tight smile of his own. "Nothing, dearest. Nothing to concern yourself about at all. Let me treat you to your bridal dinner and a bottle of the best champagne the King's Arms can produce!"

Now, here we are, ensconced in our first home in Whitechapel, a set of modest, but pleasant rooms above a greengrocer's shop. Whitechapel is not the most fashionable or even respectable neighborhood in town. Still, it is certainly a livelier place than the countryside around Longbourn. I am so very glad to be away from all the rolling hills and rambling rivers of those parts, where the social life is *so* dreary. Nothing ever happened there, except for holiday celebrations, an occasional ball, or fox hunting parties, which we never attended anyway, because we could never afford a hunter-jumper.

Here, it seems the city never rests. The air rings constantly with the sounds of carriage wheels and horse hooves on the streets, of vendors hawking their wares, and church bells tolling the time. The air also roils with acrid-smelling coal smoke; some days it's almost unbearable. Nevertheless, I love living in a city, especially one as big and glamorous as London.

Respectable or not, I am fine for now with Whitechapel. After all, I don't plan to be here long, but more on that story later. I'm feeling peckish for my breakfast, and I must go rouse my lazy housemaid, Bessie.

Chapter 2

July 1, 1814

Dear Diary,

Almost two years have passed, and I've just rediscovered you in the back of a dresser drawer. To my surprise, I find that I now have a mind to try writing in you, after all. Perhaps Mary was right. It could be enriching to record my thoughts, feelings, and experiences here.

What's most on my mind now? Why, *men*, of course!

How I do love the sight of a man in His Majesty's pinks! My heart skips a beat at the mere sight of the rich red fabric, shining brass buttons, and tight, white leggings. All the better if the man in the clothes has a square jaw, big blue eyes, and a full mane of hair—no matter what the color there—as long as there is lots and lots of it.

What a vixen these last lines make me seem. The truth is, though I love my husband dearly, I still enjoy looking at other men. What's the harm in that, after all?

Lizzie used to chide me for "this puerile obsession," whatever that means. Dear sensible Lizzie, who despite her disdain for Mama's "husband-seeking," as she put it, made the best marriage of us all, to handsome Mr. Darcy, and his even handsomer estate, Pemberley. Lizzie, who never cared a fig for fashion or flirtation.

(My, I rather like the sound of that last line. What does bookish Mary call it when you string together words that start with the same sound? Obliteration! Yes, that's the thing).

I blame Mama for encouraging me, for she clearly had the same obsession. I do believe she was more excited than Kitty and I whenever soldiers came to town. She would have us cross the street to make sure we caught their eye and gave them a saucy smile.

"You will make cheap tarts of those girls," Father warned her. Mama was having none of that, though.

"How you do go on, Mr. Bennet. They're simply high-spirited. What man doesn't admire a girl with a bit of sass?"

Father would simply groan and escape to his study. I do believe he was happier there, amongst his books and pipe racks, than anywhere else on earth. He certainly looked content when we found him there last spring with a great history volume on his lap and a big smile on his blue lips. The physician said it was dropsy, but I'm not so sure. Father was never the same after all of his girls, save Mary, left home. I think it broke his heart.

Who would have ever dreamed he would go before Mama . . . she, who has been at death's door for years? Now *that* was a shock to her constitution, to be sure. She took to her bed for days, wailing, "How inconvenient of you, Mr. Bennet! Reverend Collins owns Longbourn now, and Mary and I shall surely die homeless!"

She was wrong, however. Mr. Collins simply traded the little parsonage he and Charlotte occupied for Longbourn, and Mother and Mary are as cozy as clams in the cleric's cottage now. (There I go again! I think I have a knack for this obliteration thing. Mary is going to be so envious when she sees how literary I'm becoming).

The reverend even offered to let them remain at Longbourn, probably at the insistence of sweet Charlotte. However, Mama wouldn't hear of staying in a house where she wasn't mistress. "I may be a pauper, but I do have my pride."

She would never admit it in a million years, but I venture to say Mama is happier today than ever before. All she ever cared about was finding husbands for her girls. With Kitty's simple nuptials to her naval officer shortly before Father died, we are all well placed now—except, of course, for Mary, who seems to have embraced spinsterhood. She always gave less of a fig for fashion and flirtation than even the haughty Lizzie.

Lizzie and Darcy look in on Mama often, and have her out to Pemberley for musicales, picnics, and long, lazy visits. Eldest sister, Jane, and her kindly Mr. Bingley are a bit farther off, but they, too, are as attentive to her as they can be.

None of us ever expected it of her, but Mama has become quite the doting grandmother to Lizzie's twin boys, who are starting to walk and talk. Darcy complains that she spoils them dreadfully.

Yes, all things considered, I believe Mama is quite contented with her life and the matches we've made. However, I clearly snared the handsomest match of us all. None of the others' husbands are as comely as my George, nor cut as fine a figure in their clothes—not even the dashing Mr. Darcy.

However, I daren't wander far from George's side, for women are always throwing themselves at him. He is completely unaware, of course, so modest is he and single minded in his passions— first me, then advancement, and finally, games of chance. He's so clever at the latter that he keeps us quite well off—far, far above the norms of most officers in our acquaintance.

Oh, yes, now and then, grumpy merchants complain of unpaid bills and come to claim pieces of furniture or silverware, but George's luck always turns for the better in time. He eventually replaces the missing articles with things even more expensive than the originals.

All in all, I'm a happy girl. The weeks roll along, filled with card parties and balls, and the future promises to be even brighter. George is very ambitious, and says he will settle for nothing short of greatness.

He predicts he'll soon have his chance to prove himself worthy. That nasty little man, Napoleon, is rumored to be plotting his escape from exile on Elba, and George says he plans "to show him a thing or two."

Chapter 3

July 12, 1814

Dear Diary,

Could life be any more exciting than it is right now? Would I be boasting if I observed we seem to be the darlings of London society these days . . . at least the military side of it? How to describe all that's happened these last magical weeks?

Only a short while ago, I wrote of George's dreams of greatness. As if to prove them true, soon after that, we received an invitation to a soirée at the home of retired general Hermès Hafsted, viscount of Wexhamshire, and his famous wife, the former Madam Marie du Monde, a refugee and widow of the French Revolution. (Wexham is a small, prosperous shire north of London; their lamb is greatly prized). The invitation said that the viscountess had arranged for a conveyance to pick us up that evening at five o'clock.

The lamplighter was finishing his work, and the streets were lit with a golden glow when that conveyance arrived at our townhouse. Imagine my surprise to find it was a huge coach-and-four with four footmen in attendance, and not just any coach, but the grandest, smartest coach I have ever seen. Imagine my further surprise when we were handed in to the coach and found that there were already several passengers in it. There sat the viscountess herself, and two handsome young officers with big bolts of fabric on their laps, seated on either side of her.

"Bonjour, mes chéris," she gushed in a musical voice, greeting us as warmly as if we were old friends. "Meet my escorts, Lieutenants Messieurs Henry McBain and Martin Blake." The men smiled and nodded, though her continued chatter gave them no chance to speak.

"These gallant gentlemen volunteered to accompany me into town to shop for fabric. I simply cannot find anything in your English 'French' fashion shops that any self-respecting French gentlewoman would be seen wearing. Do you not find it curious that a country such as yours, which has been at war with France for centuries now, should be so in love with its fashions and yet also be so thoroughly unable to keep up-to-date with those fashions?"

This from a woman who obviously knew a great deal about fashion. Yet, she was cloaked at present from head to toe in a rich purple velvet cloak that revealed little but her face. She is said to have been a great beauty in her day and is still quite handsome although quite aged now—at least forty, I'd guess. Nonetheless, the little bit of face I could discern was most arresting.

She had a high, intelligent-looking brow; likewise high, wide cheekbones. Her large dark eyes snapped with vitality; they were lined with thick black lashes beneath finely arched brows. Her nose was a bit long and patrician, but nonetheless in proportion to her face, and her wide mouth with full red lips revealed perfect teeth when she smiled, which was often. The overall effect was clearly breathtaking to the men on either side of her, for they hung on her every word. As I glanced aside at George, I saw that he, too, seemed captivated by her, and I fought to suppress a wave of jealousy.

She carried on with her cheery monologue, predicting a glorious evening to come, expressing her pleasure on meeting "the promising young officer my husband is so fond of, *and* his pretty young wife."

"Ah, how my dear husband struggles with retirement, but he had no other choice. Mon Dieu, how the poor man suffers from gout! His only joy now is advising the talented young men he meets at his club. And he says *you*, Lieutenant Wickham, are one of the most promising young blades he has seen in some time . . . although he did not tell me, the jealous thing, how handsome you are!"

I had liked the gracious lady immediately, but now recognized that she was not only likable, but a keen observer of human character. My George beamed with pride at her praise, but couldn't find the opportunity to thank her before she carried on with further praises, not for him now, but for me.

"Ah, but where did you find this absolutely fetching young lady, Monsieur? She will surely be the belle of my little gathering tonight."

Now I knew that I could come to love this great noblewoman. We continued on our way, having the most pleasurable conversation, without us saying a word, until we arrived at Hafsted House.

—

As we approached the grand house by a long, tree-lined drive, we soon saw that the "little gathering" had every window ablaze with light, while dozens of carriages waited to discharge passengers at several coach blocks in front of the mansion. We, of course, went around back to the family entrance, where even more footmen hurried up to help us from the coach and escort us into the house. Once inside, we were greeted by an army of personal maids and valets, who helped us to freshen up in preparation for the party.

As a sometimes guest at Jane's and Lizzie's homes, I am certainly no stranger to grand country manor houses. Hafsted House was not nearly as large or beautiful, nor as old as Pemberley, but was still an impressive residence. In addition, it had far more servants, dressed in finer uniforms and livery than at Pemberley, and, of course, more modern furnishings. The graceful lines of their French furniture are far more to my liking than the heavier furniture the Darcy family has acquired through the generations. Alas, who am I to judge others' furniture, when we can hardly hold on to what little we have at Whitechapel?

All primped and preened, women and men alike soon thronged to the great hall, which was illuminated as if it were midday by countless chandeliers and candelabras. The air was heavy with the scents of the various perfumes and colognes guests wore, as well as the tempting aromas of roasted meat, fish, and baked goods coming from the food tables. In the corners where men gathered, talking in low voices, spirals of aromatic pipe smoke swirled above their heads.

I located George in the crowd and took his arm, for I found myself suddenly nervous. I had been pleased with my new frock, a sheer linen shift of powder blue, sown all over with seed pearls. However, the other women's finery made me feel almost shabby in comparison.

The latest French fashions the viscountess had found missing in London's shops were everywhere at Hafsted House that night. Empress Josephine had caused a scandal in Paris when she appeared in evening dress with her breasts almost visible through a sheer, tight-fitting bodice. As I glanced about the room, it appeared even our modest English womanhood was willing to risk the same scandal. Everywhere I looked, I saw the tight, high-waisted bodices modeled by the empress, in gowns of every color and fine fabric.

It took me awhile to overcome my surprise at seeing several dark-skinned women among the guests there. Wearing draped, brightly colored saris of the most beautiful silk imaginable, they mingled with the French and English guests, seeming quite comfortable, despite coming from a different race and culture.

Seeing my shock, George leaned down and explained to me that the coalition of allies Wellington formed to defeat Napoleon in the recent Peninsular War included some Middle Eastern forces. These women were the wives of those officers, whom he pointed out to me, standing across the room beside the general, nodding gravely at whatever he was saying at the time.

The men were very dark, indeed, not so far as to be Negroid, but even more brown than their attractive, paler-skinned wives. I had never seen anyone as dark skinned, and found the experience a little unsettling, yet exciting. Their exotic appearance was heightened by the unusual bloused shirts and trousers they wore and the elaborate turbans on their heads. It was indeed a varied assembly.

Standing in their midst, the general regaled them with old war stories. He was a portly, jowly man, years older than his beautiful wife, with a florid complexion that suggested a fondness for outdoor exercise (and perhaps spirits, as well). His bushy white eyebrows and thick white mustache couldn't conceal a certain sweetness in his eyes and smile . . . unexpected features for a lifelong soldier. His right foot was heavily bandaged, due to a flare-up of his gout, but he nonetheless exuded a vigorous energy. All in all, he made an imposing figure. I felt honored he had taken an interest in George.

Naturally, the most compelling vision of the evening was the viscountess herself, who staged a grand entrance, surrounded by an entourage of courtly young men. As soft string music began playing from a gallery overhead, she breezed through her admiring guests, blowing kisses and clasping hands. When she reached the center of the room, she removed a gauzy throw from her shoulders and gave it a careless toss to a nearby maid. A collective gasp went through the room.

The gown she was wearing was an exact replica of the one Empress Josephine had worn in Paris to such shock and outrage. The viscountess seemed totally unconcerned, perhaps even a bit pleased, by the whispers that rippled through the room. Finally, some bold gentleman somewhere in our midst had the presence to cheer, "Brava, Madam! Brava!"

That was all it took for the entire room to break into applause. The viscountess was soon swarmed by talkative women admiring her gown and asking who had made it for her. I started to say something to George about our hostess's audacity, but found he was suddenly nowhere to be seen. I began to wander through the room, greeting other guests and admiring the beautiful paintings and tapestries hanging on every wall.

I soon found myself drifting toward the savory smell of food at the end of the hall. There, several sideboards were laden with the grandest spread I'd ever seen. Silver salvers were stacked with shellfish and cold meats; tiered crystal pastry stands overflowed with the famous, flaky French rolls; and several iced bowls of Limoges porcelain held big, glistening mounds of black caviar surrounded by toast points. A separate dessert table offered a variety of the most beautiful pastries ever concocted, all with names I didn't recognize and wouldn't remember later.

I filled a crystal plate with pastries—tangy lemon tarts, buttery scones, rolls as light as air—and dug into them with relish. I was soon quite full and happy—until George rushed up to me and whispered, far too loudly, "Not another bite! You're making a spectacle of yourself!"

The blood rushed to my face and tears stung my eyes. A stunned silence descended over the room.

"Non, non, Monsieur!"

The viscountess rushed up to me and took my trembling arm in hers. "*Ce n'est pas vrai,* sir. It is not so. All eyes here see nothing but a pretty young girl with great *joie de vivre!* She is enjoying my food with gusto, as it is intended to be eaten. That is cause to celebrate, not chastise."

She turned and scanned the gathering. "*N'est-ce pas, mes amis?* Am I right?"

All the gentlemen raised glasses in the air and cheered, "Here, here!" The French women laughed outright at the blush now rising in George's cheeks, while the English women patted gloved hands in polite applause.

Ever the gallant, George recovered quickly and bowed with a great flourish. "I stand corrected, Madam, in the most charming manner possible, by the most charming hostess imaginable."

The viscountess extended her hand to him, and he took it and kissed it. As he did, he looked up at her with a contrite face and a dazzling smile. "Am I forgiven, Madam?"

She turned to me and winked. "I believe this handsome man of yours has a bit of the devil in him. *Mais oui?* But yes?"

With that, the room broke into laughter and the tension lifted. Guests returned to their conversations and trips to the sideboards. The viscountess took George's arm in hers.

"May I borrow your husband for a bit, chérie? I believe some of the general's guests might like to meet him. His Majesty needs clever men like this one as he prepares for whatever comes next in Europe. We may have put Napoleon away on Elba for now, but he schemes constantly to escape. It's only a matter of time before he succeeds."

She pointed across the room to a cluster of men who were chatting and swirling brandy snifters. George's eyes widened as he recognized one especially tall, handsome man. He couldn't contain his excitement.

"Commander Wellesley! Oh, *could* you? Would you? I'd be forever in your debt, Madam."

"We shall see about that," she murmured and led him away. "May I, chérie?" She called over her shoulder as they left.

"Oh—of course," I said, to no purpose, for they were oblivious to me.

Whatever embarrassment I felt at being abandoned thus soon vanished as I found myself surrounded by gossipy women. Before long, I knew more about Madam Marie du Monde than I had ever wished to know.

Chapter 4

August 1, 1814

Dear Diary,

My goodness, but servants can be tiresome creatures! I don't wonder that they all need superiors to order them about. They certainly have no initiative of their own.

The morning sun was already creeping through my drapes when I realized Bessie hadn't brought me my tray. I sat up in bed and heard the clock on the mantel chiming (noting that no fire burned in the grate, either). It was 10 o'clock. I grabbed the bell on my bedside table and rang it, forever it seemed. Still, no Bessie.

"Where can that wench be?" I wondered aloud. That's when I noticed the bedroom door ajar and heard the clatter of silver plate coming from the other side of it. I rose, slipped into my peignoir, and went to see what the commotion was—only to receive the shock of my life.

Bessie was rifling through the sideboard, putting my best silver into a sack—and the sack was one of my best satin pillowcases!

I hurried to her side to stay her hand. "What is the meaning of this outrage?" I demanded.

The insolent girl had the nerve to become indignant with me.

"An outrage for an outrage, that's what it is. I'm not bein' paid, and I can't work for free, can I?"

"You deceitful girl! Why, only last week I heard the master promise to pay you in full at the end of this week. 'On his honor as an officer and a gentleman,' he said."

She was full to the brim with rudeness, that girl. "Now wasn't that fine of 'im? I suppose he thinks I can buy bread with his empty promises—for that wasn't the first time he made me the same vow. He's been making it to me for two months now. If that's the 'honor of an officer and gentleman,' he ain't got much."

With that, I had no choice but to slap her hard. She was totally out of control, after all—but the cheeky thing slapped me back! The nerve of the girl. I have never been so ill treated in my life. I fell back against the dining room table and rubbed my cheek, thinking, What is the world coming to?

"I'll be taking myself off, now," she said, holding up her pillowcase sack. "There's only enough here to cover what you owe me, and don't even think about calling the law on me. When yer landlord tells the beadle how much rent you owe him, you'll surely go to debtors' prison . . . you and yer fancy 'officer an' gentleman!'"

She stormed out the door and slammed it so hard the whole building shook.

I did the only thing a lady can do at such times . . . crawled back into bed and cried. Then I penned a letter to Mama asking for a little loan. After that, I drifted off to sleep, wondering, "Where is George?" He didn't come home again last night—I hope it was because he was doing well at his cards.

He promised to take me to the Staffords' tonight . . . surely he won't miss the biggest ball of the season. It would do him such good to be seen there, too, as he hasn't heard anything from Wellington since meeting him at Hafsted House. There are supposed to be lots of important people there this evening. Lord and Lady Stafford know all the high-placed officers.

What a maddening turn of events: to be the toast of high society mere weeks ago, the scorn of an ignorant servant girl today.

Worse still . . . who'll do my hair now that Bessie's gone?

Chapter 5

August 12, 1814
Pemberley House
Derbyshire, England

Mrs. George Wickham
#1 Cannon Street Road
Whitechapel District
London, England

My dearest Lydia,

Mama begs your pardon for not responding herself to your recent correspondence. However, receiving it sent her into such a state that I asked if I could help. She said that I could, by answering you for her. She gave me her thoughts and feelings, and here they are.

To begin with, she sympathizes with your issues with servants. She asks me to remind you of how often she had to take to her smelling salts over some laziness, theft, or other indignity the staff imposed on her at Longbourn.

However, she grieves the fact she simply isn't able to make you a loan. She did speak to her solicitor, beseeching him to send you some funds from her endowment. She was incensed at his response; he told her she barely had enough to live on herself, much less make loans to others. She is fuming over it still. "Who works for whom here, after all? One would think it's his money, not mine!"

Given all of the above, I hope you'll not take offense at me for intervening personally here. We had an especially bountiful harvest at Pemberley last year, and my household account is quite ample right now. When I spoke to Mr. Darcy about how I should spend my little nest egg, he said, "Treat yourself to something special, for once. Do something that pleases only you." (Sometimes I marvel that the outspoken, opinionated girl I once was ever had the good fortune to find such a loving, giving husband.)

And so, dearest Lydia, I am enclosing a draught for a certain sum (I can only guess at what, in fact, you might need, as your letter to Mama simply asked for "a little loan"), and thus hope that what I have enclosed will indeed tide you over for a while. Furthermore, I insist on sending it to you, not as a loan, but as a belated wedding gift.

You may recall, our own lives were in a bit of an uproar at the time of your nuptials—I had just turned down Mr. Darcy's first proposal and was struggling with my feelings for him—so I don't believe I ever settled any kind of a decent gift on you and Wickham. Thus, this gesture is simply making up for my past negligence.

Now—a word about the vice of pride, which you know I have struggled with myself all too often. Please, little sister, don't let pride prevent your accepting this gift, which I so happily offer. I have been full of smiles and song since deciding to send it to you. It would completely break that spell should you refuse it now.

Having decided to intervene into your affairs once, I've decided to do so twice. I've taken the further liberty of asking our faithful housekeeper, Mrs. Reynolds, to contact her sister, Margaret, who is housekeeper at a large townhouse in London. I'm hoping she can recommend a dependable girl to you, perhaps even one from her own staff. Mrs. Reynolds is posting that correspondence to her sister at the same time she is posting this one from me to you. Thus, I hope that Margaret will be contacting you soon.

I have been quite the busybody lately, have I not? I admit it—and yet, it has done my heart such good to do so. Please don't deny me the pleasure of imagining you living in less distress because of my intercession.

One final item—and admittedly a delicate one—in light of past tensions between Darcy and Wickham: I need this gift to remain a secret between you and me. I feel certain Darcy would be pleased if he knew of my actions here, as he has, in fact, directed me to do as I wished with the money. However, it may trouble him to think that Wickham had control of the money, rather than you. I hope you can understand and accept this one condition I place on the gift.

Your loving sister,

Lizzie

Chapter 6

Lt. George Wickham
Brooks's Officers' Club
#28 St. James Street
London, England

George,

Where are *you?*

Things have come to a very bad pass, indeed, when the only time I see you is when I rouse in the night to find you snoring beside me, smelling of brandy and tobacco. Then, when I wake in the morning, you've already gone. Yet things have become far worse, when I am reduced to sending a messenger boy to your officer's club to communicate with you.

Enclosed you will find a correspondence of urgent importance from our landlord.

Lieutenant Wickham:

I can no longer extend your lease without payment. This notice of eviction will be enforced Monday next if I do not receive payment in full of your unpaid rent for the last three months.

As a former military man myself and a loyal subject of His Majesty, as well as supporter of his latest war against the tyrant Bonaparte, I have tried to be lenient on your behalf. It grieves me to evict another soldier.

However, it has come to my attention that you have been seen nightly at the gaming tables at your club, where it is reported your losses have been considerable of late. I cannot brook knowing that you are frittering away money you could be using to pay your rent. Furthermore, word from all the merchants in the district is that you haven't paid the butcher, the greengrocer, or anyone else for months, either. Therefore, I will be forced to have the constable remove whatever furnishings remain in your rooms next Monday if I am not paid in full.

Regrettably,

William Brookings, Esq.

So, dearest husband, what are we to do? And you are *still my dearest husband. I know how you struggle with the inactivity of being here in England when you are eager for active duty somewhere.*

Still, you cannot gain anything by spending every day drinking and gambling at your club. Lately, I have come to wonder if perhaps your superiors, seeing your gaming and drinking habits, have come to question your competency to succeed at the front.

Please, please, please come home to me soon, alert and awake, and take care of matters here.

Your loving wife,

Lydia

Chapter 7

August 18, 1814
#1 Cannon Street Road
Whitechapel District
London, England

Mrs. Fitzwilliam Darcy
Pemberley House
Derbyshire, England

Dear Lizzie,

I have received your most generous gift, and, for once, don't quite know what to say. I will admit, I was angry at first. It seemed on first consideration a high-handed, even superior gesture on your part—it was such a large sum of money, after all. The mere sight of the numbers on your cheque reminded me of how little we have, and how often and how quickly it seems to trickle away. The contrast was galling to me.

Then your words about pride struck home, and I realized I was, indeed, indulging in and even relishing it. My "anger" wasn't anger at all, only wounded pride. So, yes, I gladly and gratefully accept your gift in the spirit with which you intended it—as a gesture of love and support, not superiority.

I also accept your condition of confidentiality. I will find a trustworthy money handler, and ask that he hold and invest the *sum for me, dispensing a modest allowance to me regularly, so that I may keep us in a state fit for an officer of His Majesty's army and his wife. I will even make some small portion available to George for his cards, but only a small portion, and only now and then, claiming to have come into the money from selling some piece of my jewelry or silver.*

For, you see, despite appearances, I am not quite as silly as others think me to be. I am coming to truly know the man that I married—both his strengths and other aspects of him. I do truly love him still and pledge my continued loyalty to him. However, I no longer entertain any illusions about his character.

I hear the words whispered about me behind my back at gatherings: impulsive, feckless, immature, and gullible. I pretend not to care, but the labels hurt nonetheless, especially lately, because, as time goes by with my beloved, the words are not as true as they once were. I may have been all of those things and worse, once, but I am not the same girl now.

I have learned that every hero has his weakness. What is the Greek myth, the one about the fellow's heel? Well, my George's heel is his gaming habits. In all fairness to him, he is quite good at his cards, usually. When he stays too long at the table or has a bit too much to drink, he loses his edge—and sooner or later, some merchant is banging on the door, coming to cart away the furniture or silverware. Even a loyal wife grows tired of living in shame, of not being able to face the neighbors, or butcher, or grocer, without seeing the looks of contempt on their smug faces.

I refuse to live this way any longer and I am stronger than you think. I will make changes in the way I run my household—yes, my household, though it is for George I run it—so that he can hold his head high amongst his fellow officers and superiors, and be proud of himself, not for his looks or winning at cards, but for his achievements, and of me for helping him make them.

You will see, my older, wiser sister. I will make the most of your generous gift, and you will be amazed at all I accomplish with it.

Your "feckless" but changing little sister,

Lydia

Chapter 8

August 20, 1814
#1 Cannon Street Road
Whitechapel District
London, England

General Hermès Hafsted, Viscount
Hafsted House
Wexhamshire, England

Dear Sir,

I am astounded!

I just returned from our club where I learned that you've settled my gambling debts; also that in doing so, you specified you needed no contract for my repaying you. I am equal parts grateful, humbled, and mystified.

Friends tell me they noticed you observing me. If true, I'm not sure what that might import. Having just received this tremendous gesture of friendship from you, dare I hope it means that you have some special plans for me? Forgive me if I'm being presumptuous. I am merely trying to understand what could have motivated such generosity on your part.

You remind me a great deal of the older gentleman who raised me, Mr. Darcy of Pemberley in Derbyshire. He was like a father to me, treating me exactly as he did his own, natural-born son. When he died,

I thought I would never find another man as kind and affirming, a friend so loyal and true. Now, I believe I have . . . and I can use such a friend these days.

I like to play the part of the man who is always in control, but if I were truly in control, would I risk losing the scant wages I receive as an officer through gaming? It's a behavior I don't understand, but I'm beginning to examine it.

I sometimes feel being raised in wealth and luxury was a mixed blessing. It provided me an education and upbringing I would never have had as the son of Mr. Darcy's steward. I was fed and clothed like gentry . . . but none of the abundance was truly mine. When I was expelled from that world by Mr. Darcy's son, I had nothing. I could have pursued the ministry, as a parish was made available to me, but that life, too, would never have been my true calling. I love adventure and risk too much—the thrill of a contest, the even greater thrill of winning, and being considered the best.

Thus, a soldier's life was my choice, and I have largely been happy with that choice. However, even in this life, I encounter mixed blessings. We dress grandly, are provided ample food and housing, and are feted to grand parties and balls by the people we serve and protect. Although again, these benefits are not really ours to keep. Once out of service, we have little but our pensions, if we've served long enough to earn one; and the life a man can lead on a military pension is nothing like as grand as what we've experienced while in uniform . . . no more lavish balls or parties, no more admiring girls hanging on our sleeves.

At the gaming tables, I feel at least the promise of bettering my condition. I know it's a risk, but, as I said before, I love risk! What soldier doesn't? Usually it doesn't seem such a terrible risk, after all. I've often been told that I have an excellent head for strategy and outstanding intuition. As I watch the cards being played and the faces of the men playing them, I sometimes feel as if I can read minds and foretell the future . . . and my luck has been good for the most part.

Admittedly, I seem to have encountered a prolonged slump lately. I suppose it's my restlessness at being on furlough so long. During the Peninsular War, I felt useful, even important. Since then, I seem to have little purpose in life.

Oh, bother! Reading back over what I've written here, I see the word "feel" far too much. It suddenly occurs to me that perhaps you will find it unmanly of me to unburden to you in this way. However, I couldn't possibly accept such a generous gift from you without tendering my most heartfelt thanks and regard to you.

I'm forever in your debt. If there is ever any service I can provide for you, no matter how big or small, I will be honored to do so.

> *Your humble servant,*
> *Lieutenant George Wickham*

PART TWO

To Arms, at Home and Abroad

Chapter 9

September 1, 1814

Dear Diary,

Plus ça change, plus ça le même chose . . . the more things change, the more they stay the same.

The French have a sage saying for every occasion and I am learning all of them, like it or not, thanks to a series of unexpected happenings, all involving the viscountess.

Recently, my new maid, Clarice, brought me my breakfast tray with a calling card on it: The Viscountess of Hafsted requests the honor of calling this afternoon at one.

Panicked, I checked the clock above the fireplace where a cheerful fire burned in the grate. It was already 10 o'clock, too late for me to pen a note declining. I had no choice but to receive the viscountess.

Foregoing the tempting hot rolls on the tray (Clarice is working out quite nicely thus far), I took a few large sips of coffee and leapt from my bed. Clarice helped me into a suitable day dress, and together we went out to the parlor to set things right for a visit from nobility. She bustled about gathering newspapers and dusting, while I busied myself rearranging and fluffing cushions.

Thanks to Lizzie's generosity, I've been able to have some furniture and wall hangings returned. Compared to Hafsted

House, our modest rooms were going to seem terribly shabby to Madam, but there was no help for it. Ours was the home of a minor officer in His Majesty's army, and besides, she'd invited herself. She would have to take whatever hospitality I could offer.

Clarice was overwhelmed at hosting an aristocrat.

"Lord, lord, Mrs. Wickham, how do I talk to her? What do I call her? Yer Highness? Yer Majesty?"

I had to laugh. She's a well-meaning girl, but this is her first post as an actual maid, rather than a char girl or scullery wench. She still has much to learn.

"You address her as, 'Madam,' Clarice. That will do. Only be sure to curtsy and keep your eyes downcast when you do."

"Yes'm," she murmured, clearly agog at the thought of greeting a viscountess. I could see her out of the side of my eye, already beginning to practice her curtsy.

She's a pretty young thing, with a sweet oval face, bright blue eyes, and glossy brunette hair escaping from beneath her cap. More importantly, she has a pleasing temperament. Watching how seriously she took this new duty, I was reminded again of how lucky I was to have found her.

When we had done the best we could to prepare the simple room, I had Clarice fetch my purse, and counted out some coins from it.

"Run down to the baker and grocer, please. Get me some fruit, soft cheeses, and scones—oh, and a small flask of sherry. Be quick about it, too. It's going on noon, and what if Madam is early?"

She nodded, donned a headscarf and darted out the door. I went back to my breakfast tray, where the rolls had grown cold, but were still soft and tasty. I finished them off, as well as the cold coffee, then found myself unaccountably sleepy. Stretching out on the divan and arranging my head so that I didn't muss my curls, I fell asleep in minutes.

The next thing I knew, Clarice was nudging me awake.

"She's here, Missus, *she's here!*"

I jumped up, and went to the mirror to check my hair. "Thank you, Clarice. Give me a few moments to welcome her, then bring us the luncheon tray."

She curtsied (quite well by now, I observed), and raced to the scullery. I counted to 10, took some deep breaths and joined the viscountess in the parlor.

She had her back to me and didn't hear me enter the room. Even from the back, I could see that the dress she was wearing was expensive; it was fashioned from shimmering jade green silk, with a high collar that reached up to where her hair was tied in a chignon, beneath a smart little bonnet that perched on the side of her head. Even from the back, I could see that she was judging our sorry little home and finding it lacking. I heard her clucking and saw her shaking her head.

I was furious.

I summoned my best icy tone of voice. "I am afraid Whitechapel is no Hafsted House, Madam, so, of course, you must find it quite lacking."

She whirled to face me, a blush creeping up her neck. She covered it quickly by coming to clasp my hands and give me a swift peck on each cheek. "Ma chérie, you mistake my thoughts on your sweet abode."

She turned and waved her hand across the room. "I was thinking, in fact, what a graceful, gracious space you've created here with the simplest of adornments. These landscapes, especially, are quite nice. You have chosen ones that depict long vistas and broad expanses of countryside, giving depth to the small room. The divans and armchairs are all simple, yes, yet elegant, in lovely soft palettes and fabrics of different textures, which catch the eye and soothe the touch. You have . . . how do you English say it? *Le vision d'artiste*, the artist's vision. I do not denigrate this lovely room at all. *Mais non!* I applaud it!"

Now I was the one who found blood rushing up her neck. I bowed my head, in what I hoped was a polite acknowledgment, but was afraid to speak, fearing my voice might quaver. Fortunately, at that moment, Clarice tiptoed into the room, balancing a heavy tray, and deposited it on the low table before the divan. Once through with that accomplishment, she heaved a great sigh and looked up at me with a relieved face.

"Thank you, Clarice. That will be all." She looked even more relieved and backed out of the room, curtsying the entire way.

Madam and I took seats by the tray, and she began helping herself to food, while I poured her a sherry. I was pleased to see the tempting treats Clarice had chosen: fluffy yeast rolls, sweet-smelling currant scones, a pungent wedge of Stilton, and a golden carafe of sherry.

The viscountess, too, seemed pleased, as she dove into the tray with the same gusto I'd shown at her soirée. "You'll forgive me, ma chérie, for invading you in this way, giving you such short notice. However, I had business in town and thought how lovely it would be to see my new little friend while I was here."

I was beginning to feel guilty for having been brusque with her earlier. "Oh, you are most welcome, to be sure, Madam. It's no intrusion at all. I had nothing else to do today but write some letters, and I was dreading that, actually."

"I understand completely, chérie. There is so much to do in this world, so many things to see. Why spend life tied to a table, writing letters? Go out and live, I say."

She paused to take a sip of sherry, then gave me an arch smile. "But then, I suspect I need not say this to the young lady with such joie de vivre who graced my little soirée last month and charmed the whole gathering."

I remembered that night and the embarrassment I felt at being publicly chastised by George—hardly charming the whole gathering, I'd say—but also how grateful I'd been that the viscountess had intervened to save face for me.

"You are most kind, Madam. I won't forget how you came to my rescue that evening."

She waved a hand and sniffed. "Ah, that was nothing. We girls have to stick together, do we not? Our men, with their courtly ways and gallant talk, can be charming, it's true. Then they can be brutes, as well, n'est-ce pas?"

I nodded and looked down at my cup, unsure where the conversation might be going. She reached over and put a hand on mine. "May I speak frankly, chérie?"

I suppressed the urge to be rude and ask, "When do you not?" Instead, I simply nodded again.

She smiled and scooted an inch closer to me, her warm hand still covering mine. "I pride myself *un peu* on being a keen judge of temperament, both male and female, but male especially. I saw and spoke of it that night regarding your handsome husband, so clever and debonair, yet I could see he had a bit of the devil in him, too. Why should he worry that you ate abundantly, 'making a spectacle of yourself?' Why, his own pride was the reason. I jumped in to whisk him away where he could strut for some of the important men there, so you could feel free to enjoy yourself."

I remembered the aftermath to that scene, when a group of gossipy women came to keep me company and tell me tales about Madam's colorful background, featuring several marriages, numerous lovers, and some kind of spying. I had thought she was whisking George off to flirt with him that night. It had never occurred to me that she might be salving his pride and doing me a kindness at the same time. But why?

"Women gossip, *non?*" she said, as if reading my mind, and I blushed. She didn't seem to notice, though. "Ah, yes, we do. However, did you know that men gossip even more?"

I thought for a moment. "No, I don't suppose I did know that."

"Well, they do. The general, my dear husband, gossips like an old lady over his port some evenings, let me assure you." She ventured another sly glance at me, as if judging how frank she could truly be, then seemed to decide to go deeper.

"What do you suppose he gossips about, chérie? Why, the goings-on and the rumors circulating at the officers' club. Alas, there is a great deal of talk there, it seems, about your handsome husband. Oh, no, no, no, do not look so alarmed, my pretty. Not all of it is negative talk. I spoke the truth the night of my soirée when I said how well my husband thinks of your husband, of his cleverness and promise. However, there was concern some months back about the amount he was gambling and drinking. He was there at all hours, I'm told."

I was beginning to get very angry again. What purpose could she have in coming to worry me with troubling talk about my husband, especially when it was all in the past? I had made good on my promise to Lizzie; I'd made changes in the way I ran my home and dealt with my husband. No longer did I humor his every whim and indulge his wild behavior. I'd made it clear that I needed him home more, and that I believed his career hopes hinged on being more responsible. He had responded well; we suddenly seemed quite solvent for a change, and he was home most evenings, very attentive to me.

Madam must have sensed my feelings for she patted my hand. "Ah, I see that I have gotten your English back up, and I beg your pardon. Please do not freeze me out. I wish only to be a friend."

"I thank you for your intentions, Madam, but I don't understand how this news of ugly talk about my husband should further a friendship. Indeed, I find it most hurtful." I fought to hold back tears.

She surprised me with a nostalgic smile. "You remind me of myself, long ago, chérie. That brave toss of the head, even when you are worried, perhaps even afraid, I'd guess. Yet you have your pride. You will not let your fears show. You will stand by your husband and stand firm against the world. Brava, my dear, brava!"

I softened. "Merci, Madam, and yet, I still don't understand . . . why are you here today? Surely not merely to anger, then praise me?"

She laughed merrily. "Mais non, you dear girl, but of course not. Madam du Monde doesn't play games, although life at court may require one to learn and use them at times. Such game playing is bad here in England; it was toxic in France—toxic and ultimately deadly." A memory seemed to come to her and she shivered.

"No, I do not come merely to worry you. In fact, I hope to relieve your mind before the end of my visit today. For you see, the general and I have a plan we would like to present to you. It is a plan we must have you bless before we present it to your husband. Because, you see, we must convince your husband that this plan is in *your* best interests."

My head was spinning, and I started to protest, but she put her hand to my lips. *"Attends, ma petite.* Only listen for a while, please." I nodded, and she resumed.

"As I have said before, the general is quite fond of your George. You see, he has no heirs. He lost his only children, sons, three of them, and their mothers in childbirth, years before he met me. That is why he finds such joy guiding the young men he meets in the army. They are all his lost sons, and he has done these young men a lot of good over the years. Most of them started out as mere lieutenants, but hold much higher offices now.

"He has reason to believe your George holds special promise. Also, that he needs a father figure, as well, perhaps? I believe he was raised as the adoptive son of an older gentleman—an older gentleman who died, and whose son subsequently exiled him from the estate, n'est-ce pas?"

It was a highly abridged version of the story, but captured the gist of it accurately, so I nodded.

"C'est bon! Then we can all do each other much good! Here is what we propose. The general would like to have a man-to-man talk with your husband, to express his hopes for his future, and his wishes to help him advance up the ranks. However, he expects your George to decline his help, that his pride will prevent him from accepting help of any kind. Would you agree?"

I wasn't so sure. There was a time when I had held George in such high regard, that I would have said yes. However, the long, painful months of watching our household furnishings come and go, time and again, while he drank and gambled and ignored dire warnings from merchants and landlords had left me drained. I still loved the dear man desperately. Merely seeing him come through the door, tossing his hat across the room, and unbuttoning his crimson jacket, still made my heart flutter. If I could, I wanted to support whatever proposal the Hafsteds had come up with on his behalf.

"I suppose," I said.

"*Très bon*," she said. "Therefore, we must bypass his pride and convince him to accept our help on your behalf. The general will tell him that *I* wish to take *you* under my wing, to groom you for the life of a high officer's wife, to tutor you in matters of fashion and beauty. For you see, I have no offspring of my own, as well. The Revolution, and later, Napoleon, robbed me of my husband, and any chance of a family."

"But how?" I asked.

She gave me the same proud smile she had flashed the night of her soirée as she had thrown her wrap to her maid. "By having you come live with me as my adoptive daughter at Hafsted House. With your husband, of course."

All the air went out of me. "What?"

"Mais oui, but of course! Such fun we'll have, too—shopping, doing dress fittings, entertaining all the best people—oh, it will be grand! Meanwhile, the general and your George will be together all the time, talking horses and hunting and military matters. The general can shape and mold his nature, taming his wilder ways—be a steadying influence. I believe we can guarantee that your husband will succeed under this tutelage. He *will* achieve advancement, sooner rather than later, the general feels sure. So . . . what do you think, chérie? It will work, *c'est vrai?*"

My mind was reeling. It was such a preposterous plan and so unexpected, I couldn't imagine how to respond. I suppose my predicament showed, for Madam removed her hand from mine and put a comforting arm around my shoulder. To my surprise, the gesture wasn't unwelcome. Perhaps I needed a bit of a mother figure, as well?

"Say yes, chérie," she murmured in a soothing voice. "Say yes. What can you lose?"

She made it seem such a simple question: What did I have to lose, after all? George would have a leveling hand; we would both have a comfortable place to live, without angry merchants banging on our door; and I would have the time of my life—parties and dresses and handsome men asking me to dance—everything I'd always wanted in life.

Only . . . why did I suddenly wonder if I still wanted those things?

I have never dealt well with matters of depth, and this was becoming all too deep for me. *Enough*, I decided. I returned the viscountess's hug, and even ventured a quick peck on her cheek.

"Why . . . yes!" I declared. "Oh—yes, yes, yes!"

Sometimes short, simple actions have long, complicated consequences.

Chapter 10

September 23, 1814
Hafsted House
Wexhamshire, England

Mrs. Fitzwilliam Darcy
Pemberley House
Derbyshire, England

Dearest Lizzie,

Thank you for your invitation to the ball coming up at Pemberley. However, I'm afraid I must decline. For you see, we are hosting a ball of our own on the same night—or, rather, we are the guests of honor at a ball being given on our behalf that night. No, dearest sister, I haven't taken leave of my senses. Let me explain, starting from the top . . .

Some time ago, George attracted the attention of an older gentleman at the officers' club, retired General Hermès Hafsted, the viscount of Wexhamshire. Shortly after that, he and his wife invited us to a soirée at Hafsted House. There, George met the Commander Wellesley, and it became clear that the viscount and viscountess were prepared to take both George and me under their wings to advance his military career. The viscount has no heirs, and it appears he sees George as something of a son.

Recently, the viscountess called on me at Whitechapel and made the most extraordinary offer—to welcome us into their home, so that the *general could provide guidance to George. Despite my misgivings, I gave in, and, Lizzie, it was the best decision I ever made.*

To begin with, there are the not inconsiderable material advantages. I didn't fully realize how dreadful it was living in constant fear of raging debtholders coming to our door and demanding payment, or worse yet, carting away our furniture. It took weeks of living here to shake off the anxiety of it.

Then, too, there's the frequent company of gay and stylish people here. I also didn't realize how lonely I was at Whitechapel. Oh, yes, I had the company of my little maid, Clarice, who is a delight in every way. (Dear me—I just remembered—I never wrote Mrs. Reynolds to thank her for sending her to me. Please say something to her for me, and I'll get a note in the post shortly.) I've brought Clarice with me, of course, and it's been fun to see how she takes in all the grand people and splendor of the place.

Admittedly, Hafsted House isn't nearly as splendid as Pemberley. However, it is more fashionably furnished, with all the latest Regency furniture and gilt mirrors everywhere. I love to twirl before these looking glasses, and spin the folds of whatever lovely gown the viscountess has recently bought for me. George says I've become quite vain and spoilt, but I think he secretly likes it.

Speaking of George, oh, my, dear Lizzie, you wouldn't know the man. I think you, and even Darcy, would be proud to see the changes wrought in him, all in a mere few weeks.

He and the general are inseparable. They spend every day together, dawn to dusk . . . hunting, riding, or arguing politics and wartime strategy over chess and cards. The only troubling aspect of any of this is the talk of war, for the general says Napoleon is amassing an army from his exile.

Regarding cards, George hasn't played them with anyone but the general since arriving here—nor has he been to the officers' club except in the company of the general. Thus, the problem of him running through his pay as soon as he receives it has vanished overnight. The general has even been advising him on how to invest his money. We are now part owners with the Hafsteds of a sugar plantation on some island called Barbados. Have you heard of it?

Oh, Lizzie, I have never been as happy as this! Who would have ever dreamed I'd be living in such luxury? Little more than a fortnight ago, we were penniless—no, worse than that—up to our ears in debt. Only, don't merely take my word for it. Come see for yourself.

Please do make a visit, as soon as your ball and mine are out of the way. I'm sure the viscountess would love to meet you, and that you would enjoy her, too. She is so merry, after all; who can resist her?

I must go now. I am being fitted for my gown for the ball, and I have already kept the dressmaker waiting too long. Adieu, dearest sister and au revoir. (Goodbye until I see you again.) But I forget, you speak French better than any of us!

> *Lovingly yours,*
> *Lydia*

Chapter 11

Mrs. Agnes Collier
#10 Hawley Mews
Camdentown
London, England

Dear Mum,

   It's me, your Clarice. I guessed you wouldn't recognize the handwriting here, because it's not mine. Mrs. Ames—we call her Cook—saw me trying to write you after chores tonight and took pity on me. She said she would write down whatever I wanted to say to you and I'm surely glad. You'll remember I was never good with a pen.

   You already know that I got me a good post as a lady's maid awhile back, and that was a happy change, for sure. The missus is a sweet woman, about the same years as me, I'd guess—very pretty and good-natured—who treats me well. No orders or demands. Whenever she wants anything, she always asks, "Clarice, would you please do this or that?" Why, it's almost like she's my friend, instead of my superior.

   Her husband, the lieutenant, is a gentleman, though not as polite as she. There's something in his eyes I don't like very much—he looks a girl up and down like she's a horse he wants to buy. He's seldom around these days, though . . . always off riding or hunting with the general.

"Who is the general?" I hear you ask. Lord bless me, Mum, you'd never believe it! I'm living in a palace near as big as the King's!

Seems the lieutenant made a special friend of this important general, who invited him and my missus to come live with him and his missus, some French lady who came here during the Revolution. He's retired now and complains a lot about gout, making him seem a gruff, ill-tempered man, but that's all for show. He's very kind and soft-spoken actually, to me and all the servants.

Now his Missus, she's another thing . . . not mean or sharp-tongued so much as uppity and full of airs. She seems happiest when she's ordering everyone about, making a mess of matters, usually—that, or shopping and doing fittings for yet another gown, either for herself or my missus, who she's taken a shine to, like the general has to her husband.

I'm not sure I like the hold Madam has on her. Seems she's teaching my missus a lot of bad habits, if you ask me . . . how to play cards, make idle chatter, and butter up the men—that and spend way too much time in front of mirrors for my liking. The missus is a lovely thing, to be sure, but she doesn't need to be primping at her reflection, day in and day out. It can go to a girl's head and make her vain—like the general's wife. And I do like my missus so, just as she is, or was when I first went to work for her . . . cheerful and saucy and full of life.

But who I am to judge? I'm only a servant girl, who should mind her own business, which right now is heading upstairs to help the missus to bed.

I'll try to write, or rather, ask Cook to help me write you again soon. Till then . . .

Your daughter,
Clarice

Chapter 12

October 1, 1814
Hafsted House
Wexhamshire, England

Sir Arthur Wellesley
Wellesley House
Wellington, England

Dearest Wellington, you old dog,

Grand to see you in London last week! What a lark, going shopping with the wife, and running into you. I'll be damned if that woman doesn't have more clothes than the Queen herself. Still, she looks so fine in them I can't say no to her.

I was delighted to hear you have an assignment for my young friend. The lad has worked hard to become a better man. I can assure you, his drinking and gambling days are done.

I can also assure you I have every confidence he can now handle any task you ask of him. The wife agrees with me here, by the way. No one has ever beat her in chess but young Wickham. She thinks it's because he has such a brilliant grasp of strategy, and she should know, having survived the Revolution in France without losing her head.

You said you cannot share details because all is mum in this matter. I won't challenge you on that point, but dare I venture a guess? I'll wager it has something to do with making sure a little "French Frog" *never runs rampant across Europe again. By George, it's got to be that. Am I right? Am I not? However, I know you won't say. Ha, ha, aren't you the crafty one?*

Per your orders, I'll not say anything to the young man until you give the word. Till then, I'll spend every moment I can with him. Having lost my own sons years ago, I seem to have been blessed with a new one, here late in my life, although what a bittersweet gift it is.

No one knows better than you and I that war is hell, and when young men go into it, very few of them come out of it intact. Even if they survive physically, often they're not the same men. I cannot bear the thought of losing this new son, and yet, it is what he wants, to prove himself in battle.

While we can hope our putting Napoleon away on Elba ensures a time of peace, we all know how crafty he is. God forbid that he does escape, for if he does, it's only a matter of time before he'll bring war back to Europe, this time with a vengeance. We will need brave and steadfast men like young Wickham in leadership when that time comes.

Keep my young friend in mind for advancement, will you, my good man? I'd stake my life and name on this claim: whatever you ask of him, he will not let you down.

> *Your obedient servant,*
> *Hermie*
> *Viscount of Wexhamshire*

Chapter 13

October 12, 1814

Dear Diary,

How long it seems since I've written anything in these pages, and how much has changed since I did. Looking back at previous entries, I realize how young and foolish I was at the time. Though only a few months have passed, I feel much older, sadder, and, I suppose, wiser now.

Once I swooned at the sight of a man in uniform. Now it only brings me pain. George leaves soon on some hush-hush assignment, so secret that he can't tell even me—his own wife—about it. I have no idea where he is going, or what he will be doing. How silly is that?

He is in uniform constantly now, looking more dashing and handsome than ever in the crimson tunic I once loved to see, but it now only reminds me he will be gone from me soon. Who knows when and—dare I even say the horrid word—*if* he will ever return to me?

Worse yet, he's in constant company of the viscount and viscountess, talking in hushed tones about something or other I'm not allowed to hear. It's most vexing. I'm not ashamed to confess that, were the general not present at these rendezvous, I'd suspect the viscountess had romantic intentions for George.

Poor dear, he's always had no sense whatsoever of how attractive women find him.

Speaking of George, I haven't seen him all morning. I think I'll go track him down and make him take me for a walk. It's a glorious autumn day, and I won't have him here to promenade me about the grounds much longer. Oh, dear, there I've gone and made myself sad again.

Chapter 14

October 20, 1814
Hafsted House
Wexhamshire, England

Mrs. Fitzwilliam Darcy
Pemberley House
Derbyshire, England

Lizzie,

Come quick, sister! I need you here desperately. My heart is broken, and I have no one else to turn to save my loyal Clarice, who is way too sheltered to grasp a matter such as this.

This place that I thought a haven has become a snake pit!

Oh, the betrayal, the infamy of it, and at the hands of people I loved and trusted. The general and viscountess I can write off as acquaintances I believed in too soon. But George! The husband I've stood by and saved from debtor's prison, pinching pennies and placating grocers and landlords! How could he do it to me?

What's more, I've learned he's been lying to me about another betrayal for years. Last night, I overheard him in conversation with the general. He disclosed that Darcy paid him a sizable dowry for me. I thought that George married me for love. He's certainly professed that to be the case all this time. To find that I was paid for like some slave or indentured servant, well, it's . . . it's so demeaning.

I need you to come get me, sister. I need the sanctuary of Pemberley. Surely, George won't try to approach me there, not with Darcy at hand, considering the antipathy they have for each other. I can't bear the sight of him and have kicked him out of our bedroom. He professes his innocence, but I can never trust his word again.

In closing, I repeat, help me, Lizzie, please.

Lydia

Chapter 15

October 28, 1814
Hafsted House
Wexhamshire, England

Mr. Fitzwilliam Darcy
Pemberley
Derbyshire, England

My beloved husband, Fitzwilliam,

How I miss you, dearest . . . your strength, your sweet smile, your warmth beside me in the night, and, right now, your wise counsel.

I have been with Lydia for five days now, spending almost every moment together. She is beside herself with grief and rage, and I have striven hard to soothe and support her. How I've wished you were here to advise me. Let me tell you what I have done and hear your thoughts on my efforts.

She is eating a bit now, though when I first arrived, I was shocked by her gaunt appearance. She admitted she hadn't slept or taken sustenance for days. How she was still standing, I have no idea.

As you guessed when you read her summons to me, she believes Wickham has been unfaithful. She thinks the viscountess 'beguiled and seduced him,' inviting them to come live here for that express purpose, through a ruse about the general counseling and guiding him.

I have mixed feelings about the latter point. Admittedly, the viscountess is a most beguiling creature, and we both know Wickham's unsavory history with women. However, as to the matter of the general's guidance being a ruse, I believe not.

You wouldn't know George, husband, if you spoke to him today. He has a wholly different demeanor about him . . . calmer, more confident—I'd almost say dignified. He drinks almost nothing at all anymore, and his gait and gaze are steady.

I have not been able to speak at length with him or with our host and hostess. However, when I have spent time with them, I saw what I believe to be a truly heartfelt affection and respect amongst the three of them. The general calls him 'son,' and I believe he genuinely sees him in that light.

As you know from Lydia's letter, she has asked us for sanctuary. Here's where I need your advice most, for I have declined to give it to her. (I can almost see in my mind's eye your combined surprise and relief to hear that.) Let me explain, and then you can tell me whether I've been a wise counselor or not.

After days of rain, yesterday's weather was fine. I cajoled Lydia into taking me on a tour of the gardens. We set off with the lunch basket Cook had made for us and ambled about the place all morning. (It is lovely, by the way, though a bit excessive for my tastes—overblown, elaborate, and clearly designed to impress.)

We made our way through the park to its focal point, a grand Gothic gazebo, replete with gargoyles and spires (a ghastly thing, actually). We brushed fallen leaves from our seats and delved into our basket of savory meat pies, tea biscuits, and crisp fall apples. Lydia went straight for the sweets, while I enjoyed a pork pasty.

She got right to the point. "When can we leave for Pemberley?"

I hedged. "Tell me more about all that's happened."

"*I already have. George and that woman have been having an affair. I'm sure of it.*"

"*How?*"

"*I came upon them, time and again, with their heads too close together for propriety's sake. They were always playing cards or chess together . . . that and talking about the French Revolution, her role as an agent for the Crown, trying to free the king and queen, and how she barely escaped with her life. She makes herself out to be quite the brave heroine. Such an imposter!*"

"*How do you know that they were intimate?*"

She dug into her reticule, produced an envelope, and spilled out its contents, some pieces of torn paper. When she was done assembling a puzzle of sorts, I read these cryptic words: "an intriguing plan . . . cannot say no . . . no one must know, though."

"*What is this?*" *I asked.*

"*Proof of their affair, of course! I found George writing a letter in the library. When he saw me, he tore it up and tossed it in the fire— then he said he had an errand to do and rushed from the room. These few bits of papers fell outside the grate. What else could they be but a love letter?*"

I took her hands in mine and tried not to sound like a patronizing older sister. "*Dearest one, it could have been dozens of things. Have you asked him or the viscountess?*"

She sniffed. "*Why give them the chance to tell more lies? You can't imagine how awful it's been, Lizzie. The man I love more than anyone else in the world, a woman I admired and trusted . . . for them to have . . . to have . . .*"

With that, she collapsed, sobbing, into my arms. She wept for a long while. Finally, she rallied—she's always been a plucky girl—and raised swollen eyes to mine.

"What should I say to them? What should I do?"

I fought the urge to tell her. It's all too tempting to play the wiser one, fixing other's problems—and to take pride in that, as well—but then they never learn how to think for themselves.

"I believe you already know," I said.

She frowned. "Me? Why, I don't know anything! You always say and do the right things—it comes to you naturally. Whereas I stumble about like the fabled bull in a china shop, making people angry, or, worse yet, making them laugh at me."

"Posh," I said, hugging her. "They're merely jealous of your vitality."

That seemed to give her pause. "Joie de vivre," she murmured. "That's what the viscountess said I have."

"Exactly," I agreed. "Yet, you are much more than that, little sister. Surely you must know that of all our siblings, you're the smartest and most talented?"

She was incredulous. "Such lies, Lizzie! I can't stand any more lies!"

"It's true! When we were young, engaged in sketching or painting, you were always done first and had the best colors, perspective, and likenesses."

She smiled. "That's what Madam said about our rooms in Whitechapel. That I had an artist's eye."

"It's true. How about when we went shopping together? You always knew right away what ribbons and fabric you wanted, and what colors suited your complexion best . . . while the rest of us dithered about, and usually came away with something that made our skin turn green."

That made her giggle at last. Then, she sobered. "But I am feckless too, am I not? Admit it, Lizzie, I've heard it all my life."

Time for the awful truth. "Yes," I admitted. "They do say that; and so you are, or, rather, have been at times, a bit . . . impulsive. But it's only your youth, and your love of adventure; and you are much more mature now than you were even a year ago."

She seemed to mull this over. "I said as much in my diary recently."

She sat in thought for several moments, then threw me a suspicious glare. "What about the other betrayal: George concealing from me that Darcy paid him a dowry to marry me? Did you know about it, Lizzie? And, if so, why didn't you tell me?"

I felt my face flush, but owed her an honest answer. She'd been lied to enough. "I did know, sister, yet felt that I had no other choice but to keep it from you. What good could it possibly do for you to know that? Look at the hurt it's caused you now that you do know it."

She seemed a little mollified. "You were sparing my feelings?"

I nodded yes, and she sighed. "Well, that helps a bit; although, I want to know, why does everyone always keep things from me? It's as if people think I don't have the sense or strength to face the truth. Then again, I suppose that's what I deserve for behaving in a feckless manner. My goodness, how I'm coming to hate that word."

Her face softened. "I suppose there's another way to look at the whole matter. Darcy might have paid George to marry me, but he couldn't have paid him enough to stay married to me, 'feckless thing' that I am. Could he?

I ventured another hug, and she returned it warmly. We sat for a while in silence, until she leveled a steady gaze at me. "You're not taking me to Pemberley, are you?"

"No," I admitted. "God knows that I want to, sister. Except it's not what would be best for you. It's only what would be easiest for you. You have a husband here, who, despite his faults, loves you deeply; and he is growing as a man, into a much better person. I can see the general's impact on him; it hasn't been a ruse. What would happen to *him and to you, do you think, if you simply run away from all of this unhappiness and confusion now?"*

She collapsed into my arms, in tears again. "Oh, Lizzie, why does it have to be this hard? Why can't love be fun and easy? Why do we always have to be working at life?"

I stroked her hair. "I don't know that we do, dear. Maybe we're better served to take things as they come, and do whatever feels best at the time."

We sat like that for a long while. Then she raised her head and squared her shoulders. "Come, Lizzie. Let's get out of this ugly place. I need to talk to George and Madam."

And that, dear husband, is what happened next. I don't know what was said, as she didn't ask me again for guidance, nor did she report on what transpired afterward.

However, I will add this: Lydia and Wickham sat next to each other all evening, holding hands or stroking each other's cheeks, and the viscountess and general were both in high spirits, seeming much relieved to have peace again under their roof.

I'll close this now, and begin packing to return home tomorrow. I look forward eagerly to hearing your opinions of me.

> *Your loving wife,*
> *Lizzie*

Chapter 16

November 1, 1814

Dear Diary,

Sister Lizzie just left, and I already miss her dreadfully. Who would have ever dreamed that she, the most sensible of all our sisters, would ever be so dear to me? She always disdained me as silly and frivolous. Now, it appears she holds me in higher esteem than I thought. Such a lot she's given me to contemplate . . .

She actually thinks I'm smart! At first, I thought she was teasing me or placating me to coax me out of my distress. Yet she persisted, reminding me of talents and skills I possess that show another kind of intelligence than that of people who read books. I suppose it does take some sense to pick the right colors and textures for a frock, or to execute a proper portrait, or a watercolor. I'd simply never thought of it that way before.

Still, why can't I be smarter about people? It seems that there, too, I am always drawn most to that which is pretty, only to find later that what's *inside* the person isn't as pretty as the outside.

Take the viscountess. She's a famous beauty, who turns heads even at forty, but who also has a shallow side—too concerned about appearances, her own and other people's. To her credit, she did show greater character than I expected when I confronted her with my suspicions recently. I take some pride in having figured out how to handle her and that awful situation.

I found her in her dressing room, ordering her maids about in search for a misplaced gown—there were probably hundreds there. As soon as she saw me, she began blinking rapidly, uncharacteristically nervous all of a sudden. She covered it quickly, though.

"Ah, my little friend," she purred. "I am glad to see your walk and talk with your sister has revived you. The general and I have been so worried about you."

I squared my shoulders and thrust out my chin. "There is only one thing about me that need worry you, Madam . . . how fast you can get away from me if you ever make advances on George."

Her face paled and she started to sputter something, but I cut her off.

"This is not a conversation, Madam. It's a declaration. There is nothing more to say on the topic, so I'll bid you good day."

I wheeled and left the room, taking pleasure in slamming the door. (Ever since, she has treated me with a newfound respect.)

Then there is George to consider. The first time I laid eyes on him, I literally lost my breath. He is so uncommonly good-looking, tall and muscled, with ruddy cheeks, and sparkling dark eyes and hair. Moreover, he is always smiling, always making light of things, so that it's constant fun to be in his presence. I see the admiring and jealous glances of other women whenever we are out together.

I sometimes marvel that we ended up married at all. When we first met, he seemed more interested in Lizzie than in me, and I was pursuing one of his friends. Eventually, events brought us together, and it was exhilarating to be with him—for a time. Then came "the dark ages," as I've come to think of those days at Whitechapel.

I had to come to terms with this truth in those days: George is not a man of strong principles. Oh, yes, he strives to be accomplished and acknowledged for doing good things, but he relies too much on the praise of others, particularly those in positions of power. He dreams of greatness, and perhaps he does have it in him, after all. Sadly, I have not seen it flower yet, though I am encouraged by recent events.

After confronting Madam, I sought out George in the library. He was smoking and playing chess with the general, who, like his wife, paled a bit on seeing me. George, too, eyed me with caution. I was thrilled. I had never had any intimidating influence over others, and, now that I did, I found it intoxicating.

"May I speak to my husband alone for a moment, sir?"

I didn't have to ask twice. The general muttered something about finding a better pipe, and almost ran from the room.

George came and tried to embrace me, but I held him at arms' length.

"I'll make this brief, then we'll never speak of this again."

He eyed me even more warily. I had never spoken to him thus, and he had no idea how to deal with my new assertiveness.

"Of course, my love. Whatever you say."

I squared my shoulders. "I know now that Darcy paid you to marry me—a considerable sum, too, and that he paid off all your gambling debts, as well."

"Darling, please it wasn't like that at all."

I held up a hand to stop him. "All I need to know is this: Have you gotten your money's worth? Are you happy with the deal you struck? Or have you tired of the toy that was bought for you? Perhaps you've found another toy to entertain you?"

I never expected what happened next. Hearing my stinging words, George's eyes welled with tears. He came to embrace me again, and this time I let him, though I refused to embrace him in return.

"Dearest Lydia. Can I ever heal the pain I've caused you? You, a total innocent, wanting nothing more from life but affection and fun? Yes, I was encouraged to wed you by Darcy, but that's all his settlement was—an inducement. I loved being with you from the moment we met. Such laughter, such gaiety! When you seemed to be taking an interest in me, I was the happiest man on earth. When you sent a message to me that you were in Brighton and wanted to see me, I couldn't believe my good fortune. Nothing like that had ever happened to me before, a woman being so bold and making it so plain that she wanted to be with me. I admired your courage tremendously."

"Everyone else found it scandalous," I murmured into his chest, beginning to soften toward him a bit.

He hugged me tighter. "Not I. I thought it was the bravest thing I'd ever seen—I, a soldier, who's been to war. I thought to myself, 'I *have* to be with this woman. She is the most amazing creature I've ever encountered.' I felt even more strongly when we retreated to the King's Arms in London, and I found you to be such a . . . well, affectionate creature, as well."

I blushed at the memory of those early, halcyon days. Could I have ever been such a minx?

"So, yes," he continued. "I am well pleased with 'the deal' I struck. Whatever brought us together, something much more now holds us together."

That was exactly what I needed to hear from him, but still I was unresolved.

"There is one thing more," I said.

He put his hand under my chin and raised it so that I could meet his eyes. "No, there isn't, my love. There is only this one thing, you and me. There has never been another woman, and there never *will* be."

That did it for me. I melted into him and hugged him back fiercely.

—

So where does that leave me now? I have a husband who is far too handsome and ambitious for his own good. I have a comfortable—no, make that lavish home, thanks to the good graces of two wealthy benefactors. I have a family, and one sister, in particular, who love and support me, no matter how foolish I might be. I suppose there is nothing more I could wish for.

Only . . . why am I still so sad?

Chapter 17

November 9, 1814
Hafsted House
Wexhamshire, England

Mrs. Agnes Collier
#10 Hawley Mews
Camdentown
London, England

Dear Mum,

It's me, your Clarice again, though I expect by now you might recognize Cook's handwriting.

It's curious times here at Hafsted House lately—on the face of it, happy things going on, but underneath, a feeling something is wrong, and I don't know what it is.

We are beginning the holidays, which I'm told are grand here. The Hafsteds always host a Guy Fawkes Day party for the entire village, with a big bonfire; this year, they had fireworks, too! I never saw the likes of them . . . so pretty, though the noise scared me half to death. Every man, woman, and child left with some little gift . . . oranges and toffees for the little ones, tins of coffee, tea, or tobacco for the grown folk.

In a few weeks, Cook says, we'll start making puddings to store away, soaking in rum till Christmas; also, taking baubles and beads out of storage to weave amongst the evergreens the gardeners will cut for us to decorate bannisters and mantels.

If only my lady were happier.

I've learned so much about serving my betters since coming here—how to arrange flowers, set a table, turn down linens, and all the rest—but I haven't figured out how to comfort one's betters.

It is such an awkward thing, to be dressing a lady's hair and see tears trickling down her cheeks. How can any Christian serving girl not address such a thing? But Mrs. Graves, the housekeeper, says it is absolutely forbidden to pry into our superiors' private matters.

Some amongst the staff think my missus is none too bright and over dramatic. I disagree; she seems wonderful smart to me—always cutting up and making clever comments—well, except lately. She's generous, too, often giving me her cast-off frocks, which, though old to her, are quite the nicest dresses I've ever owned. I wear them to church every Sunday, and the other girls are very envious.

Don't worry, though, Mum. I won't let having fine things to wear go to my head, nor get all vain and uppity. You taught me to know my place, and I do.

Cook says she needs to lay out things for breakfast tomorrow, so I must close this letter now.

As always . . .

Your daughter,
Clarice

Chapter 18

November 12, 1814

Dear Diary,

It's come at last, the day I've been dreading for months . . . George leaves tomorrow on the assignment he's been given—I still don't know what it is, but I've begun to piece some ideas together.

It would all be much nicer if he were sad to be leaving me, but he is chipper and cheerful, going about the house, whistling and humming military marches. I suppose that's to be expected, now that he's been promoted to colonel, and given an important assignment. He is fit to burst with pride, as am I, in truth.

Still, sometimes I want to choke him!

Madam has redeemed herself a bit in my eyes, reminding me that this is what soldiers do, go to war and leave their families behind. If we, their loved ones, are fortunate enough, they come back to us, alive and intact. That thought gave me chills and made me feel pangs of guilt.

She also reminded me that I, too, have a job to do—letting him go as gracefully as possible and making his remaining time here pleasant. That, I believe I have done quite well. He has spent every evening with me, and sometimes the Hafsteds have joined us, as well, but he has given me his complete attention, providing me no reason to suspect anything going on between him and the viscountess.

It has almost seemed like our honeymoon, and, in fact, even better, for that time was marred by the fact we'd eloped, and Darcy came after us. George has been so tender and thoughtful with me, more than ever before, that I have come to believe Lizzie's observation that he is truly a new man. He is surprising me in other ways, as well.

As usual, he still spends most of his days with the general. Recently, I passed the library where they were sitting and smoking. I heard them talking to each other in some guttural foreign language.

"Wie geht's, Herr Hafsted?"
"Wie geht's, Herr Wickham?"
"Sprechen sie deutsch, Herr?"
"Ja, ich spreche sehr gut deutsch."

The viscountess startled me, creeping up behind me, and tapping me on the shoulder. When I turned to her, she put a finger to her lips and pulled me down the hall a few steps.

"What in the world is going on?" I whispered. "What language is that they're speaking?"

She gave me a conspiratorial smile. "It's German, chérie, but mum's the word, do you hear?"

"I don't understand. George is terrible with foreign languages. Why would he be learning Prussian?"

She put a hand on my shoulder. "The Prussians are no fans of Bonaparte. They were instrumental in defeating him during the Peninsular War. Now it is rumored he is plotting to escape Elba, and it is only a matter of time before he remounts his efforts to conquer all of Europe. We need to be strengthening our ties with allies, preparing to thwart Napoleon before he gets too far."

"That's the assignment George has been given? He's going to Prussia to prepare for another war?"

Her eyes widened. "You are too astute, my dear, and ask too many questions. Some things a soldier's wife is not permitted to know, especially if her knowing them might put her husband or his assignment at risk."

I shivered at the thought and nodded my assent.

"Only know this, my curious little cat . . . your husband has been honored with a very important task, one that will give him the chance to prove himself invaluable to Wellington and the Empire—and make him a hero."

She tiptoed away, putting a finger to her lips again.

Or make him a martyr, I thought with dread, and hurried to my room to have a good cry.

I couldn't indulge in tears for long, though. Wanting to keep things cheerful for George, I put on a brave face—he was leaving in the morning, after all. That evening, we supped and played cards with the Hafsteds. I indulged in several glasses of wine, which I seldom do, and even George had a rare glass or two.

By the time we reached our boudoir, I was feeling a bit amorous. Modesty forbids me saying more than that here. Suffice it to say, I sent George off to sortie with his new Prussian friends a very happy man . . . while I took to my bed to mope for days.

I wonder when, if ever, we shall meet again—and I hate, absolutely *hate* that nasty little man, Napoleon.

Chapter 18

January 1, 1815
United Kingdom of the Netherlands

Mrs. George Wickham
Hafsted House
Wexhamshire, England

Dearest Moppet,

I know you don't like that nickname, but indulge a lonely soldier, will you? It reminds me of how you wake up in the morning, shaking your curls and running your fingers through them—ending up looking like one of the rag dolls the little girls here carry. I think often these days of how you wake up in the morning—especially that last morning we shared together. Now I imagine I've made you blush!

I hear you asking: "Where is 'here?'" Regretfully, we may not disclose our location to loved ones. It could jeopardize future transport or battle plans.

However, you can be sure that I am receiving your letters and cherish every one of them. Continue sending them to the adjutant's office in London, and they will continue forwarding them to me here by special courier. I will respond to all that I can in the same way, though I must beg your pardon for being such a poor correspondent.

I will make this excuse: I have never been as busy in my life! The work is never ending, but endlessly satisfying. I am making good *progress toward the goals that brought me here. Again, forgive my vagueness. If I write anything more specific, the letter will never make it to you.*

The men I am working with are even more driven than I am. We are gradually overcoming our language barriers and understand each other most of the time. Now and then, I say something wrong, which they find terribly funny. However, turnabout is fair play, and they soon say something in English which I find equally funny.

Other commanding officers are stricter with their men and would never stoop to joke with them. I am certainly very demanding with mine when it comes to fully discharging their duties. Yet, I think it is good for morale to be able to share a laugh with them now and then. It seems only right that a man would fight harder for a commander he likes than he would for a man he fears. Based on their readiness to laugh at my poor Prussian, I believe my men do like as well as respect me.

Despite these light moments, I am deeply impressed by the courage and conviction of these new friends. When the time comes for us to fight beside each other, I feel sure they will comport themselves with honor and bravery.

It will take all of that and much more to defeat Bonaparte should he manage to launch another onslaught, as is predicted. In his assault on Russia, the man and his army were ruthless, wreaking havoc across Europe, leaving nothing but death and destruction behind them. He never stopped to see to the needs of the citizens of whatever city or region he had destroyed—setting up hospitals, or clinics, or soup kitchens to feed the starving—but charged on to the next conquest, creating ever more suffering and starvation. Thank God, the wily Russians managed to trick him into venturing too far, too late into their brutal winter, or they and all of Europe would be French subjects now.

He can and will be defeated. The men training alongside me here now will do it. Have you ever known a Prussian, dear? I must see to it that you meet one someday. They are even more stubborn and willful than you.

Before you tear this teasing letter to shreds, let me tell you how much I love and miss you. Now that we are apart, I realize how much time I have wasted with you, how much more I could have done to show you that I cherish you, and how much work I have to do when I finally return home to make up for my many character flaws.

I have not been a good husband—or friend—to you, but I will be a better one when we meet again. Please believe that and let me prove it to you.

Your loving, though errant, husband,
George

Chapter 19

January 21, 1815
Hafsted House
Wexhamshire, England

Mrs. Fitzwilliam Darcy
Pemberley House
Derbyshire, England

Dearest Lizzie,

Oh, sister, I can scarcely contain my joy! I am with child! I'm a bit unclear as to how far along I am, but have consulted the viscountess, who believes it to be somewhere between two and three months.

As the only one of our sisters who has had children, I come to you now—as always, it seems—needing your advice. So many questions!

To begin with, when does one let her husband know? When he is there with her, I imagine a wife has no need to inform her husband of her condition . . . or would she? Do husbands and wives speak openly of such things amongst themselves? Or is it considered too indelicate? Oh, dear, I wish Mama had a better head on her shoulders and wasn't so flighty, otherwise I'd ask her these things. However, as it is, I feel sure that the mere mention of my condition will send her into one of her spells, and she'll take to her bed for weeks.

At the very least, sister, can you advise me on this? When a husband is away, at what point should his wife write and let him know she is carrying his child? Is now too soon? What if, God forbid, I should lose the baby?

For once, Madam is uncharacteristically reticent and unhelpful. I suppose that's due to her having lost her own family in the Revolution, then having married the general later in life, after he had lost all of his own family, as well. Though she tried her best to seem excited for me and said all the right words of encouragement, I thought I saw a certain pained look in her eyes, as if the mere thought of talking about having babies was hard for her. Perhaps she regrets having none of her own? Ah, but enough about that one!

Oh, what to ask next? So many, many questions, the mere thought of writing them all down gives me a writer's cramp. Why don't you come visit me again here, Lizzie? I know that it's an inconvenience, especially in the winter when roads are wet and rutted, but surely, I shouldn't be riding long distances in carriages in my condition. Isn't that right?

Oh, do hurry, dear sister, to write and tell me you're on your way. We'll stay up late every night talking, and you can tell me everything you know about having babies and child rearing. It's going to be such fun!

Au revoir.

> *Lovingly yours,*
> *Lydia*

Chapter 20

January 28, 1815
Longbourn
Meryton Village
Hertfordshire, England

Mrs. George Wickham
Hafsted House
Wexhamshire, England

My dearest, darling baby girl,

Such joy, such rapture! To know that my baby is having a baby of her own!

Lizzie shared your letter with me the other day, and although, of course, I'm delighted, I must say, I can't imagine why you didn't write to tell me, your mother, first? But, never mind, about that now. This is supposed to be a happy time; don't feel guilty on my account. I've been hurt far worse than this and am known far and wide as a forgiving woman. I'll rise above this wound shortly.

You must write and tell me all the news. Are you sick in the morning yet? Be prepared: you are going to be sick in the mornings, sometimes all day. I was wretchedly ill with your sister, Mary, the whole nine months, retching and cramping, and retching and cramping! I wanted to die. I was fine after she arrived, and I had a few weeks in bed to recover. Mr. Bennet always said that my morning sickness with Mary is what made her such a mirthless creature. However, I think it was his mother, who had exactly the same pessimistic nature—nothing at all like me.

I'm sure no such thing will befall your bundle of joy, unless, of course, he or she develops colic. There is nothing worse than a colicky baby. Kitty had it her whole first year, and not a soul in the household got a decent night's sleep that year. I didn't mind, though. We mothers do what we must to raise our children; no sacrifice is too great—and we had a most capable nursemaid.

Do you have a good midwife? You must make sure you get a good midwife. Find an older woman, one who has had lots of experience. You don't want some young thing who's only been at it a while. You recall my friend, Mrs. Porter? Her daughter had a young midwife who dropped her baby when it came out.

As for the matter of pain, don't believe any tales you might have heard about how excruciating labor is. It is quite ghastly, of course, but if you are lucky, it won't last too long . . . although it usually does with a first baby. I was in labor for two whole days with your sister Jane. If it hadn't been for a drop of laudanum now and then, I would have died from the pain alone. Naturally, I bore it without complaint, for that is a woman's lot, is it not?

Rest assured, you will not be alone throughout your coming ordeal. Lizzie is on her way to see you now, and she says she's prepared to return again and again, if need be—you know, in case there are complications of any kind, although we must hope and pray that there won't be. Keep a positive outlook, dear. That's what I do.

I, too, plan to be there when you deliver and hold your hands through the whole thing. Of course, once the baby's head breaches, I won't be able to stay in the room. Things can get pretty gruesome from that point on, and you know how delicate my constitution is.

It simply wouldn't do to have your poor old mother fainting on top of you, would it? Ha, ha! There's a funny thought, eh?

Well, Mary has brought my breakfast tray here to my bed, where I've been since I heard you were expecting. Now, please, don't worry about me. I'm sure that it's nothing serious—probably only the shock of knowing you confided in your sister first, rather than me . . . but, then, I've already put that out of my mind completely. You must do the same.

All my love and kisses,
Mother

Chapter 21

February 20, 1815
Wellesley House
Wellington, England

The Honorable Hermès Hafsted, Viscount
Hafsted House
Wexhamshire, England

My old friend Hermès,

It's always a pleasure to hear from you, and, no, I wasn't put off in the least by your bringing a "domestic matter" to my attention. After all, what are friends for? Although, as you said in your very apologetic letter, yes, there are certainly more pressing matters on hand presently than the matter of a missing soldier. Bonaparte continues conspiring from Elba, and it is only a matter of time before we will be at war again.

As to the matter of your missing friend, Colonel Wickham, I have heard back from his commander, and, no, he is in fact not missing at all. His commander writes that he is reporting quite faithfully for any and all duties; also that his unit is the strongest one there, and his men seem to like and respect him greatly.

Which leaves the question, why is he not responding to his wife's recent correspondence?

You write that the little woman is in the family way for the first *time, and that she has communicated this to her husband. I'm a soldier, not a midwife, but I wonder if the fellow isn't a bit daunted at the idea of becoming a father, especially when he's far away from home. Perhaps he's taking a little time to get used to the idea, before writing back to his wife.*

However, I wouldn't be completely honest with you if I didn't add this; there is another aspect to this story—one that I hope we can keep between us. As you well know, sometimes men away from their wives develop a roving eye. Wickham's commander admits that the man is a favorite of the ladies, and that there is one in particular with whom he has been seen quite frequently. She is not a "camp wife," so to speak, as the colonel apparently sleeps in the barracks with his men. However, word is that the woman is clearly in love with him, regardless of whatever feelings he might have for her.

Rest assured, the commander has chastened the young man and reminded him of his duties. Your little charge, his wife, should be hearing from him soon.

And that, I predict, will be the last you hear from me for a long while. We are girding our loins for battle any day now. May God save the King and protect us all.

Your obedient servant,
Arthur Wellesley

Chapter 22

February 23, 1815
United Kingdom of the Netherlands

Mrs. George Wickham
Hafsted House
Wexhamshire, England

Lydia dearest,

Dear God, what a thorough cad I've been! Can you ever forgive my not answering your latest letters, especially since they contained the blessed news that we are going to be parents? I have no acceptable excuse. I can only throw myself at your mercy and hope you can find it in your heart to look beyond this shameful behavior on my part.

Are you feeling well? Are the Hafsteds looking after you? Have you felt the baby kick yet? It seems to me I've heard that boy babies kick harder in the womb. Please let me know if that is the case.

Also, please know that I will not only answer every correspondence you send me, but initiate more letters myself in the time to come, at least, as long as I'm able to. We never know from day to day when we may be on the move. Napoleon is said to be poised to resume hostilities any time now.

I know that you hate it when I speak of these matters, especially now that you are carrying our child. But I am a soldier, dear, born to fight and defend. We have been drilling forever, it seems, and debating

strategy and battle plans in meeting rooms and pubs, on chalkboards and paper. Enough talking and planning. It's time for action!

I am impatient to move into this next chapter of my life—our life—and to show you and everyone, what I am capable of as a soldier, as a leader, as a man.

Do not fret for me, Little Moppet. I couldn't resist using the nickname again. I suppose soon it will be Little Mother instead?

I will write to you again tomorrow. I promise.

> *Your loving husband,*
> *George*

Chapter 23

March 10, 1815

Dear Diary,

The worst has happened . . . Bonaparte is free again, and Europe is at war once more. How I worry about George!

He has been much better about writing the last little while, but his letters are airy and inconsequential, giving me no idea what's really going on at his end, or what's really on his mind. In fact, they give me the distinct impression that he's keeping things from me. What that might be, I have no idea, but I always assume the worst. He has been far too full of unpleasant surprises these few short years we've been together.

Madam and the general are kind and generous hosts. They fuss and fidget about me all the time now. Marie seems to have resolved whatever difficulties she might have had with me being with child and is quite the mother hen these days. Sister Lizzie has been to see me twice now and pronounces me "the prettiest new mother-to-be" that she ever did see.

During her last visit, Lizzie thought that she felt the baby moving, though I have felt only the vaguest of flutters now and then. I would like to be able to write George soon that I've felt a good solid kick, signifying we're having a big, lusty boy. Perhaps in the next day or two?

When I ask him, the general is glib about what to expect next from Bonaparte. He puffs on his pipe, swirls his brandy, and utters meaningless reassurances.

"Don't you worry your pretty head about anything, young lass. My friend Wellington is the finest soldier that ever lived. He'll have Napoleon and his nasty little French cockroaches squashed before you know it."

Why is it men always assume women can't bear to hear the truth—that we're so weak and frail we'll swoon at the mere whiff of anything negative? I suppose it could be because of women like Mama, who literally *do* swoon at the slightest provocation.

Not me! I want to know the truth. I have to know the truth. It makes me crazy to sit and wait for the proverbial other shoe to drop.

I will write Lizzie tomorrow to see if she can't get some honest answers from Darcy about what lies ahead. He is well connected with all the biggest military sorts, and he doesn't consider all women fools. Yes, that's the answer. I'll write to Lizzie tomorrow.

Chapter 24

March 23, 1815

Dear Diary,

There's an old saying: "Be careful what you wish for." And I know now what it means.

I wanted to know the truth about what was happening presently in Europe. At Lizzie's behest, Darcy sent me a frank summary of things as he saw them. The gist of it—not good. He predicted Napoleon would waste no time reclaiming his throne and waging war across Eastern Europe.

Today's papers from London report he returned to Paris three days ago and regained control of France. He is gathering strength to overthrow Louis XVIII and already has considerable manpower and resources.

In response, England and our allies are forming a Seventh Coalition to resist him. Good heavens! A seventh! How many is it going to take to do away with him once and for all?

It appears things are moving very rapidly toward open conflict. I know that George will be playing a part in all of this. He probably already has had a hand in it; I remember all the whispering and secrecy that went on here. However, his letters continue to be breezy, conversational notes with little detail beyond humorous goings-on amongst his men in the barracks.

I finally got the opportunity to tell him what he's been wanting to hear: the little one in my womb is kicking up a storm. He has quite interrupted my sleep the last several nights, but it's a loss of sleep I welcome. Oh, would that the old wives' tales about boy babies kicking harder is true. I would love to give my darling George a male heir.

Chapter 25

April 1, 1815

Mrs. Agnes Collier
#10 Hawley Mews
Camdentown
London, England

Dear Mum,

Cook has been kind enough to write you another letter for me. I'm sorry for not writing you more, but it has been very busy here lately.

I'm sure you've heard the news of war coming again in Europe. The missus has been worried sick about it. She is with child and beginning to show a bit, though she doesn't eat near enough for a lady in her condition, in my humble opinion. Most of the trays I take to her room she returns uneaten, saying, "It just doesn't taste good." She is quite thin and wan, despite the little bump in her belly.

I believe the problem is nerves. I sleep these days in an anteroom off her suite and hear her pacing the floors all night; that, or crying out in her sleep, probably from bad dreams about harm coming to her mister.

You had twelve children, Mum. Can you tell me how to get my missus to eat? Are there certain dishes or foods that appeal to women in her way? Surely, it can't be good for her or the baby for her to be losing weight, rather than gaining it now.

Other than these worries, life is good here. I keep learning so much about service in a big house. Some days my head spins with all there is to know and do. The hardest of all is how to address the various grand folks who come to visit . . . dukes and duchesses, earls and their ladies; admirals and generals! I can never keep them all straight.

Missus says it's best I simply call all the gentlemen "Sir," and the ladies "Madam" or "Miss." That seems to have worked pretty well, so far.

Lord help me if the King and Queen ever visit. I'll have to hide in the cellar!

I need to go turn down the bed linens soon, so I'll close this letter now. If you can send me some ideas about how I can better take care of the missus in these delicate times, I will thank you kindly.

Till later then . . .

Your daughter,
Clarice

Chapter 26

April 12, 1815

Mrs. George Wickham
Hafsted House
Wexhamshire, England

Lydia, my little love,

This message must be brief, for it's happening at last. My men and I are moving out.

We knew something was coming soon when we were all outfitted with new boots last week. Although we're an infantry brigade, as one of the men's commanders, I'll be on horseback.

I've been issued the most beautiful bay gelding to ride. He's a Groningen, one of the Dutch Warmbloods—big, sturdy horses derived from the kind of stock medieval knights used to ride. Imagine that, darling. Your husband is riding a knight's mount into battle. Surely, I will be invincible astride a mighty horse like that, surrounded by the bravest soldiers ever born.

The Prussians are known for their courage and were vital to earlier efforts to defeat Bonaparte. While not particularly imaginative, they take orders well and will fight to the death for their homeland and comrades. I feel lucky to have been appointed to lead these valiant men, many of whom have become like brothers to me—although they still tease me mercilessly about how I "sprechen sie deutsch."

I confess, I will never be fluent, but I can shout, "Auf geht's," well enough. It's a battle cry, which means, "Let's go!"

Speaking of going, it is time for me to do that now, dearest. I know that your beautiful blue eyes are full of tears as you read these words, and I grieve causing you any sadness, especially these days, when you are carrying our son. However, I have studied and prepared all my life for this moment. It is what I was born to do.

I know that all you want is for us to be together. I want that too, but please don't begrudge me the pleasure of getting to fulfill my life's dream—going into glorious battle and defeating, once and for all, the most despicable despot ever to plague Europe.

That's it. The bugler is calling us to assemble. I won't write for a while, but I will have you in my heart for the duration.

> *Yours forever,*
> *George*

Chapter 27

April 12, 1815

General and Mrs. Hermès Hafsted
Hafsted House
Wexhamshire, England

Dearest Madam and General,

This message must be brief. We are pulling out, and I have already stolen too much time writing to Lydia.

You have both been incredibly kind and generous to us—there aren't sufficient words in the English language to convey how grateful I am. How did a scoundrel such as I ever stumble onto such undeserved luck? Yet, I am writing here to ask even more of you—for Lydia.

I have not been a good husband to her—I admit it freely, though with great shame. In various ways that are both known and unknown to you, I have wronged her, time and time again. I hope to be able to make that up to her when I return home. Meanwhile, it comforts me to know she is safe there with you.

I know you, General, understand the risks I face. I, who have always loved risk-taking, find I don't love this particular risk. Recently, I find that I have no vision of the future, and that troubles me. I don't know what to make of it, other than to chalk it up to the qualms all men feel when going into battle. Only I don't remember having such qualms during the Peninsular War.

Whatever lies ahead, I ask that you continue to be a father and mother to my little wife.

But I must go now. With deep affection, gratitude, and respect—
Your loving son,
George

PART THREE

A Time for War, a Time for Healing

Chapter 28

May 12, 1815
Hafsted House
Wexhamshire, England

Mr. Fitzwilliam Darcy
Pemberley House
Derbyshire, England

Dearest husband,

Oh, Fitzwilliam, what awful news I bear. Lydia lost the baby and may yet lose her own life.

The little dear was a boy, an exact miniature of Wickham, perfectly beautiful, albeit stillborn and blue. Lydia, of course, is beside herself. The midwife is giving her laudanum, but whenever she wakes, she asks to hold her baby. When she remembers what's happened, her grief is inconsolable. To hear her keening would break your heart—as it's breaking all of ours.

I have never felt so sad and helpless in my life, for I have never seen anyone as sad and hopeless in my life. Still, the viscountess says that before I arrived, Lydia called for me as often as she did for Wickham. Thus, I suppose there is some good I can do here, and I will remain as long as she needs me.

The general tells me Wickham will be hard to reach, even by special courier, as his unit is on the march, preparing to meet the French in *battle soon. May God protect Wickham—Lydia will never survive another loss.*

The only bright spot to this sorrowful situation is that it's given me the opportunity to know the Hafsteds better. I can honestly say that I like and respect them deeply. Any lingering doubts I might have had about them have been thoroughly dispelled. They both clearly love Wickham and Lydia, as well, and think of them as their own children. Their grief at the loss of the baby is almost as deep as Lydia's.

Given the circumstances, it appears that it may be weeks, or even longer, before we're able to get word to Wickham about what's happened. Assuming, God willing, he survives whatever lies ahead, how horrible it will be for him to know he has lost a son. Despite the history of friction between the two of you, do you think you could bring yourself to be involved in getting word to him somehow? It may be easier for him, hearing it from a man.

I must close this now. I am writing at Lydia's bedside, and she is beginning to stir. Soon, she will begin asking for the baby again.

God help us all.

Your adoring wife,
Lizzie

Chapter 29

June 8, 1815

Dear Diary,

I have finally found some useful purpose for the demon, Bonaparte. He is giving me an armed escort to find my George.

What a nightmare life has been since I last wrote in these pages. I still awaken most mornings as if coming out of a fog. There is a brief time while I am drowsy where I feel the baby kicking, and I reach down as I always did to pat him through my belly. Then the truth comes back to me, and I want to die . . . until I remember that George still lives and loves and needs me.

That is why I am on my way to him now.

I have much to report from the last several weeks. I don't remember exactly when, but at some point I came to, knowing the baby was gone, grieving as deeply as ever, yet ready to resume my life. Lizzie was there with me, as I clawed my way out of the abyss, and her strength, love, and wisdom pulled me through. Eventually, I persuaded her I was well enough to fend for myself, and sent her back to Pemberley—for I had formulated a scheme.

I had decided I would join George. I didn't know how, but I knew that I *would* do it. Yet, I couldn't hatch any sort of plan with Lizzie here. She knows me too well—she would have figured out I was plotting something, then dissuaded me from being "feckless."

I bade her goodbye and began to spin my web. Eavesdropping on conversations between the general and Madam, I learned that they both knew far more about current events on the continent than they let on, where Napoleon was headed—the Netherlands—and how our troops and allies planned to engage him.

My loyal little Clarice snuck into town and sold some jewelry for me. Then, with those funds, we found a confederate in one of the gardeners. He helped us arrange for a coach to Dover.

Just as we arrived there, a full moon broke through the clouds, casting a brilliant silvery light over the famed white cliffs. It reflected off the chalk palisades for miles, far out across the waves. The sight gave me hope, as if a beacon was lighting my way to George.

From Dover, we crossed to the nearest French port of Calais, on a fishing sloop manned by a very nervous crew. They muttered the whole way about "them murderous Frenchies," predicting we'd all be marched to the guillotine as soon as we landed. Of course, no such thing happened.

We found an unoccupied seaside villa on the outskirts of town with a private slip and pier. Clarice and I disembarked there at dawn and regained our land legs. Then we walked into town, arriving in time to buy a light breakfast of some rolls, fruit, and cheese from street vendors. My French was never good, and it suddenly occurred to me we might be in danger if we revealed we were foreigners in a France that was now at war. I was relieved when we were able to get what food we needed largely by pointing and gesturing.

As we sat in a little park, eating our breakfast, Clarice noticed an older woman staring intently at us. She was dressed in what appeared to be expensive, although garish clothes, and wore a great deal of face paint. We tried to ignore her, but her gaze was so keen, that I finally felt I had to say something.

"*Comment puis-je vous aider?*" I asked if I could help her.

She seemed glad I had broken the ice and approached us with a wide smile.

"*Vous etes Anglaise, n'est-ce pas?*"

Clarice gave me an anxious look, but I decided to risk telling the truth.

"*Oui, nous sommes Anglaise,*" I said, admitting that we were English.

"I knew it! I've a very good eye for strangers." Her English was good, although heavily accented.

She sat down beside us, uninvited. "What are two pretty English girls doing unescorted here? This is a very wicked town."

I decided it was a good time for some *partial* truths and concocted a story that might give us safety there even though we were citizens of England.

"I have come to find my husband, a soldier in Napoleon's army. We were married last year in London, before the resumption of hostilities. He came home to Paris last winter for his mother's funeral and was conscripted. I managed to find passage here and hope to track him down."

She whistled through her teeth. "Mon Dieu, you're a determined one, aren't you? There's a war on, you know. Bonaparte has left Paris and is on the march as we speak, on the way to the Netherlands, they say, to vanquish the English there. How do you propose to find one soldier in the midst of thousands of them?"

I sighed. "I have to admit, I haven't quite figured that part out yet."

She gave me a speculative look. "What lengths are you willing to go to?"

I assumed she was asking me about money and became fearful of being robbed. Clarice and I had a great deal of money sewn into our garments.

It was as if the strange woman could read my mind. "Relax, chérie. I'm a wealthy woman. I have no designs on whatever paltry funds you may have on hand. It's only that I have an idea about how you might find your husband."

"Oh, please, please tell me!"

She sidled up closer, and put a hand over mine. "Come with me and my girls. We leave tomorrow to entertain the troops."

I glanced again at her clothes and heavy face paint, and realized I was in the company of what mama would call "a soiled dove."

She was watching me closely, as if continuing to read my thoughts. "Yes, you have guessed correctly. I am a whore and proud of it. I run a fine, clean establishment with only the prettiest, healthiest girls. They say war is hell, but not for the likes of us. War is the best money in the world for whores. We follow the boys, camp nearby, and give them some comfort before they die. The commanders look the other way, because we keep morale up. Most of the commanders come to us, too."

She laughed at that thought. I was half appalled, half enthralled. I had never heard anyone speak so openly about things I'd been bred to consider shameful, even depraved. I liked her candor and heard the sense of what she was saying. On the other hand, I was shocked to think she might be trying to recruit us.

"Surely you can't possibly think that I . . . that we . . ."

She laughed heartily. "Oh, no, no, no, chérie! No offense, but you're not the right type. A little too . . . what's the word? Oh, never mind. No, I was only offering you a safe, sure way to reach your man. Of course, if you choose to show your thanks by paying me a little something, I wouldn't say no."

For some strange reason, I felt stung by the news that I wasn't "the right type" to be one of her girls. What did that mean, after all? Still, I decided it best to leave that question alone.

"Oh, please, Madam, yes. Please take us with you. We won't be in your way. We'll be easy to have along. And by all means, we will pay you. Only let us know how much."

She took my hands in hers and squeezed them gently. "Let's not discuss unpleasantries like money now. We'll come to some mutually agreeable sum later. For now, only know you have found a new friend. Madam Marjorie du Monde, at your service."

I started at the mention of the name, but managed to conceal it. Surely, it must be a common one in France? Besides, she was all business now, getting up, leading us away, and making plans for our departure.

"The emperor has a head start on us, but we are closer to the Netherlands here than he was in Paris. If we hire a fast coach and four, we could link up with him at the border, then keep his men company on the way to wherever they're headed."

I tried to show my interest, but my head was swimming by then. The last few days had been so strange.

And that, dear Diary, is all that I have energy to report for now. My hand is cramping and I need to sleep.

Chapter 30

June 8, 1815
Hafsted House
Wexhamshire, England

Mr. and Mrs. Fitzwilliam Darcy
Pemberley House
Derbyshire, England

Dear Lizzie and Fitzwilliam,

It's with the deepest sadness—and, yes, shame—that I need to forward you the following note:

Dearest Madam and General:

Words can't convey how grateful I am for all you have done for George and me. I will always be in your debt. However, I must leave you now, hopefully to return with George at my side. Please don't try to come after me. I do not want to be found. The only thing in the world I want right now is George. And I will find him.

God bless you and keep you—Lydia

Despite her insistence to the contrary, we, of course, mounted a thorough search for her. To our great consternation, we learned that some of our own people had aided her in her escape. Naturally, they have been dismissed.

Here's what we've been able to ascertain thus far. She and her maid made their way to Dover, where they paid local fishermen to take them across the channel to Calais. Some of our mutual "friends in high places" still have underground operatives in France. Through them, we've learned that the young ladies were last seen in a public square, in the company of a local "madame." The three went off together after a brief discussion. Now, the madame and her entire entourage have cleared out. The house is boarded up, and there's no sign of our girls anywhere. Word is, the madame has gone off to join the French troops on their march to war. We can only assume the worst—that Lydia is with them.

The wife and I are beside ourselves with grief and humiliation. We only ask that you please believe, we had no idea that the girl was healthy and determined enough to take off on such a journey.

That said, we will continue to have our operatives track her and report any news to you as soon as we receive it.

Your obedient servant,

Hermès Hafsted

Chapter 31

June 12, 1815
Charleroi Village
Kingdom of the Netherlands

Dear Diary,

Well . . . so far, so good. We have made it to the Netherlands and successfully intercepted Bonaparte's army yesterday at the French border.

Madame and her "girls"—which is how she refers to the women with her and how they refer to themselves—have been sweet and considerate traveling companions. I was raised to believe that fallen women lead sad, sorry existences. That is certainly not the case with this troupe. On the contrary, they seem endlessly merry and adventuresome creatures, constantly making jokes and telling randy tales on each other.

To be sure, some of their stories have been a bit shocking, for poor Clarice particularly, who's never been with a man and knows nothing about their appetites. I had only to raise an eyebrow at them and nod toward Clarice, for them to understand that they needed to censor themselves a bit. There's not a rude, insensitive one in the bunch.

Wherever we've traveled, they've always made sure that we had the most comfortable seats and beds. Several of them slept on the floor the first night so that Clarice and I could have a mattress. Whenever we've stopped to eat, they've always made sure that we had the first and best servings of food.

All they've asked in return was to hear our stories of "life in the big houses." Most of them come from humble origins and have little education or exposure to culture. They've listened dreamy-eyed while I described formal dinner parties, balls, and garden weddings.

Even shy Clarice has ventured a tale now and then about life in the servants' quarters. The girls seemed to take special interest in these, and one of them finally revealed why.

"Do you think the likes of us could ever land a decent job like that?"

She asked the question in a timid voice with none of the jaunty humor she and her sisters normally showed the world. I was surprised, because it had never occurred to me that someone might consider service a desirable occupation. Then I realized that, for the starving pauper, becoming a garbage picker would be a desirable occupation; and that for the garbage picker, becoming a servant somewhere clean, dry, and warm would be a desirable occupation. Similarly, it made sense that a woman who made her living pleasuring men with her body might consider being a maid a far preferable job.

This cheerful group of girls never bemoaned their lot. Judging from their many ribald tales about the men they entertained, they seemed to have thoroughly embraced it. However, that didn't mean they couldn't dream about bettering themselves someday.

I was moved almost to tears at this revelation. Looking around the circle at the girls' pensive faces, I saw that several of them were too. They had all been so good to us. I had to reassure them.

"Of course you could," I said firmly. "Just write to me whenever you're ready, and my benefactors and I will find you a good position. They know all the best people in all the big houses."

That brought a round of relieved smiles.

Then Madame laughed. "However, please, just not yet! Genevieve is one of my most popular girls, and you'll bankrupt me if you steal her away from me now. Or any of the rest of them for that matter. We're about to become rich from all the men around here."

That got the group laughing again, and the subject soon turned to bawdy stories once more. Bawdiness was their bread and butter, after all, and they were never merrier than when they were engaged in it. They might aspire to a more respectable life when their youth and looks began to fade, but for now, they did their jobs well.

It was somewhat . . . *awkward* our first night there to be camped so close to their "business dealings." I had no idea the French were such vocal lovers. Clarice was quite pink in the face until she finally grew tired enough to drift off to sleep, in spite of the noise.

However, there will be no more of that, for the near term anyway. We have already begun to hear cannon and musket fire. The countryside here is a lovely, hilly farming region dotted with dozens of small pretty villages. The French and English armies are positioned closely throughout the area. Itching for the more deadly battle that's sure to come soon, they satisfy themselves for now with taking shots at each other's encampments, or wresting roads and farmhouses back and forth from each other.

We have seen the hated Bonaparte several times. He gallops his white stallion from village to village, rallying his men, issuing orders, and conferring with his generals. I had no idea he was that tiny. Even on horseback, it's clear the man is no taller than Clarice or I. Perhaps that's why he's so power hungry, to make up for being little.

Men! I'll never understand them.

Chapter 32

June 12, 1815
Pemberley House
Derbyshire, England

General and Mrs. Hermès Hafsted
Viscount and Viscountess of Wexhamshire
Wexhamshire, England

Dear Marie and Hermès,

My husband asks that I write you for the both of us, as he is on his way to find Lydia now.

Of course, we bear no enmity toward either of you. None of us could have seen this coming. Although I am the one who most should *have*, as I am the one who is most familiar with Lydia's impulsive, stubborn nature. However, as Fitzwilliam and I learned years ago, why vie for the larger share of blame? Self-flagellating serves no purpose, except to make an already difficult situation worse.

Fitzwilliam wanted me to offer you some new information he's acquired. He has some operatives of his own in France and the Netherlands, and has been receiving frequent updates from them. As a result, he feels he has a good idea exactly where to find Lydia. Unfortunately, that is in the Netherlands, in the midst of a looming battle, the likes of which he says the world has never seen.

I shudder at the thought, and pray that he reaches her in time. Meanwhile, rest assured I will keep you abreast of any news I receive, as I know you will do likewise in return.

Your loyal friends,
Lizzie and Fitzwilliam

Chapter 33

June 19, 1815
Convent of the Recollets
Nivelles Village
Kingdom of the Netherlands

Dear Diary,

It is over . . . the battle, the war, Bonaparte's tyranny . . . and my life. Where to begin?

The easiest part is the military story.

The French started things off on the 16th, winning two battles, at the nearby villages of Quatre Bras and Ligny. There, they routed thousands of Prussian troops (yes, Prussians, my George's men), who fell back to join Wellington outside the village of Waterloo. Sometime on the morning of Sunday the 18th, Napoleon engaged the English there with all his might.

At that point, the Madame's troupe, Clarice, and I were still camped outside Charleroi, a safe distance from the front. However, we might as well have been right in the thick of it, for I have never in my life heard so much cannon and gunfire, and shouting and screaming of men and horses. I expect to have nightmares about the latter the rest of my life.

The ground shook all day, as if we were having an earthquake. Chimneys on nearby farmhouses toppled and masonry walls cracked with the vibrations. We were glad we were in tents, which merely waved in the hot, smoky wind blowing off the battlefield.

The air was heavy with the sulfurous smell of gunpowder and some other strange scent I faintly recognized but couldn't name. One of the girls came up and sat beside me as I was drinking a cup of tea to settle my nerves.

"Do you know what that smell is?"

When I shook my head, she replied, "It's blood. A great, great deal of blood. From the horses, mules, and men."

I shivered and clutched my shawl about my shoulders.

Despite that morbid moment, Marjorie and her girls have continued their tender care of us. A few of them had been through battles before and were very helpful, describing what was probably going on and telling us what to expect either way, whether Bonaparte or Wellington won. They made clear that as non-combatants we had little to fear. They were only partially right about that.

By evening, it was clear that Wellington had prevailed. The French were in full retreat, running for dear life past our camp on foot, or galloping at breakneck speed on some of the few surviving horses. Many of these men had injuries, but none so bad that they couldn't run or ride. Observing that, Marjorie made an announcement that surprised Clarice and me, but not her girls.

Rolling up her sleeves, she called to our coachman to hitch up the horses, then turned to us. "You know what's next, ladies . . . time to find the nearest convent."

I was perplexed at first. Was she planning to repent of her wicked ways and take vows with a religious order? One of the girls gave me an indulgent smile.

"That's where they'll be taking the wounded and dying. We'll be needed as nurses. Do you have any problems with dead people, dear?"

I was too frightened to admit I didn't know, that I'd never seen any.

As if they'd done it a dozen times, the whole group fell into action, taking Clarice and me along with them: tearing petticoats into bandages, collecting lotions and creams, and filling baskets with tinctures or bottles of brandy. Soon, the carriage was ready and we piled into it with our goods. No matter that it was pitch dark, save for the fires still burning far off on the battlefield. The madame and her girls, including Clarice and me, were off to be nurses.

As we passed through Charleroi, we learned from a tavern keeper about the Church and Convent of the Recollets in Nivelles, a few miles north of Waterloo. He told us that the Recollets were an Order of Franciscan friars and sisters. They were sure to be operating a hospital, he predicted.

Fortunately, the road from Charleroi to Nivelles was clear of combat. We made good time to the church, an old Romanesque structure, which was the centerpiece of town. It was also the center of the most dreadful scene of carnage imaginable, lit now in the darkness by dozens of torches.

Everywhere we looked lay bloodied men, some completely covered in gore. Some stood, leaning on big sticks made into crutches, while others lay uncovered on stretchers or pallets. Many were missing one or more limbs, some an eye or ear, some all of the above. And every single one of them, it seemed, was crying, and pleading for help—some even calling for their mothers.

Adding to this chaos and cacophony, the bell in the great tower tolled incessantly, calling more wounded to the hospital—a doleful sound that added to the sense of calamity. Looking at how many casualties were already assembled there, I couldn't imagine how any more could possibly be treated.

Like a field marshal, Marjorie herded us all into the church. There, we encountered sights, sounds, and smells even more horrendous than what had greeted us in the courtyard. The horrors there seemed all the more horrible because of the ironic setting—a peaceful place of worship, filled with crucifixes and statuary.

The sculpted figures gazed down on the crowded nave with placid faces that belied the awful scene. I was touched when several of our girls crossed themselves before a Madonna and Child.

The space was filled with writhing, moaning men. The sanctuary overflowed with pallets and even straw beds on the flagstone floor, bearing the wounded and dying. The stench of the men's blood, sweat, and excrement assailed our nostrils. I thought for a time I would surely be ill, but somehow managed to overcome my nausea.

Marjorie found several nuns who gave us instructions. We divided up, going to different areas of the makeshift infirmary: some to process new arrivals and assess their injuries, others to assist with surgeries—mainly amputations, others to clean and bandage lesser wounds, still others to cover the dead and oversee their removal.

We worked all night, without food, water, or rest. Yet, somehow, none of us seemed to tire. I suppose the sheer gruesomeness of what we were seeing and doing energized us in a strange, contrary way. Then it happened.

An exhausted nun called me to help her with a grievously wounded man. His English uniform was drenched with blood and his heavily bearded face was totally covered with it.

"Here, take these scissors and cut off his tunic, while I clean his face and see to this gash on his forehead."

I went to work, trying to cut through the sticky, wet wool, but it was hard going. As I worked, I noticed a pretty young woman nearby. She was kneeling at the foot of his pallet, rocking back and forth, praying in Prussian. I glanced at the nurse.

"His wife. Sometimes they're determined to follow their men."

I felt a wave of compassion for the poor thing, to be that young and dealing with this hell. I looked at her again and felt even more sympathy for her, as I realized that she was pregnant, and quite far along. I looked back at the nurse just as she finished cleaning the man's face.

It was George.

Chapter 34

June 20, 1815
Convent of the Recollets
Nivelles Village
United Kingdom of the Netherlands

Mrs. Fitzwilliam Darcy
Pemberley House
Derbyshire, England

Dearest wife, Lizzie,

I have found her and the little maid, Clarice, too. Rest assured they are safe and well, at least physically. However, both have undergone great hardship and stress, and, in Lydia's case, real trauma. For you see, she found Wickham . . . along with his pregnant "wife."

He lies near death, barely clinging to life in the convent hospital here. Despite her broken heart, your sister will not leave his side. Her loyalty is boundless. How she does it, I'll never know—nor how she finds it in her heart to be loving to the little Prussian girl, Brigitta, who believes she is Wickham's wife. Lydia is even trying to learn some Prussian, so that they can communicate with each other.

George goes in and out of consciousness. The attending nuns say it is only a matter of days. He lost too much blood and has some indeterminate internal damage which appears to be going gangrenous. Lydia and the Prussian girl keep vigil on either side of him, each *holding one of his hands, talking, singing, and praying over him, night and day.*

I must close this now. I am going to the infirmary, determined to persuade your bullheaded little sister and her new friend to take a break while I watch Wickham for a bit.

I need to tell him how much I admire him and thank him for his service.

Word is, that he and his stalwart Prussians saved the day for Wellington.

> *Your devoted husband,*
> *Fitzwilliam*

Chapter 35

July 1, 1815
Brussels

Dear Diary,

How long it seems since I last wrote in these pages, and yet it's only been a few weeks. I suppose that's because so much has happened in those weeks that they seem longer than they really were.

I write these words from a grand hotel in Brussels. The sumptuous setting bears stark contrast to the deathly landscape we left behind us. Darcy has been better than an angel to all of us. He has sheltered and nurtured us in every way imaginable. I feel guilty that I ever found him stuffy and dull. He is totally the opposite. But I lose track of events. Time to finish the story and retire this diary, too, I think.

We lost George one week ago. How he held on as long as that, none of us will ever know. The nuns said it was because he had "things to take care of." I think perhaps they were right.

The last day, he came to with a clarity we hadn't seen before. Brigitta and I were both there as usual, each holding one of his hands. He looked at her and then at me and then he looked totally bewildered.

"How can this be?"

"That we know each other?" I asked.

"Yes," he said. "You're not supposed to . . . this wasn't supposed to . . ."

"It doesn't matter," I said, kissing his forehead. "We *do* know each other. That's all there is to that."

He glanced at my waistline and managed a weak smile. "Our baby has come?"

I felt a knife in my heart.

"Yes, and he is well," I lied. "I couldn't bring him here, of course. He is with the Hafsteds, who love him as their own grandson."

"Ah, yes, that's as it should be," he said, breathing hard. He closed his eyes and seemed to struggle for words.

"Lydia, dearest, I'm so sorry . . . so terribly sorry, that I . . ."

I put a finger over his lips. "Hush! There is nothing to be sorry about. We have had a grand adventure together. You became the great war hero you always wanted to be, and while I may not be the great lady I always wanted to be, no one will ever call me feckless again! Our time together has been a glorious success."

Thinking of our time together made me nostalgic. The grim setting melted away, and I was transported back through the years. Hoping to comfort him, I reminisced awhile.

"What a lucky girl I was to find you. I saw an officer in the village market one day who was wearing His Majesty's pinks . . . the handsomest man I'd ever seen. I said to myself, 'I *must* have that man for my own. No matter what it takes, that man will be mine.' Oh, yes, you buzzed about Lizzie for a while, and I buzzed about some of your fellow officers. Fate finally brought us together though, and you have been mine ever since, just as I resolved you would be."

He squeezed my hand, and sighed. "Yes, but what about—?" He nodded toward Brigitta.

For some reason, despite the sad place and circumstances, I found myself tickled. "Well, there has been *that* aspect! I didn't realize at the time I was going to have to share you!"

He didn't have the energy to laugh, but did smile and squeeze my hand again.

He continued to focus on Brigitta. "What's to become of her? Poor innocent wretch."

Before I knew what I was saying, I blurted out, "She's coming with me."

His brow creased. "You would do that? For her . . . for me? After we—"

I shushed him again. "Be still. Do you think I could abandon a child of yours?"

He sighed with relief, and brought Brigitta's hand to his heart. "*Sei artig. Deh mit ihr.* Be a good girl. Go with her."

Her eyes widened and she threw me a panicked look. I reached across the counterpane and took her free hand in mine.

"Bitte?" I said. "Please?"

She gazed at George a moment, then bit her lower lip, and nodded. We remained in place that way, our joined hands forming a circle.

A long interval followed, while he dozed, and his breathing became more ragged. Finally, he came to, and looked at me with love.

"Oh, Lydia," he whispered, as his eyes began to glaze. "Not a little moppet, anymore, but a great lady, indeed. A great lady who—"

He stopped in mid-sentence and fell into a fit of coughing. When it was over, he exhaled his last breath.

Brigitta burst into tears and threw herself across his body; whereas I, somehow, couldn't cry. He looked so beautiful, lying there with his face in repose, out of pain at last. Save for the gash on his forehead, he was the same handsome officer I'd seen back in the village. Brigitta had shaved him every morning, and his high cheekbones and chiseled jaw were smooth. He was almost flawless.

Suddenly, the tone of Brigitta's wailing changed. She grabbed her belly and doubled over. "*Mein baby bekommen*," she cried.

The pallet next to George's had recently been emptied by another death. Several nuns rushed to Brigitta and placed her on it. I sat frozen beside George, still holding his lifeless hand. The nurses fashioned a privacy screen around Brigitta, and for the next several hours, the cries and groans of the wounded men in the hall were drowned out by the cries and groans of a woman in her first labor.

Sometime during the night, an elderly nun with a kind face approached me. She cupped my chin in work-worn hands.

"Perhaps we should let the aides take your husband away?"

"No!" I protested. "He would want to be here for the birth of his child."

She pointed to all the beds filled with injured men and the straw mats on the floor where still others lay. "Do you not think he might prefer his bed go to someone who needs it more now?"

I felt a flush rising in my cheeks, for she was right. Still, I couldn't seem to release his hand. She gave me an indulgent smile.

"Let me help," she said and gently extricated my fingers from his. When she was done, I found I could cry at last. She took me in her arms, gently stroking my head, while I sobbed into her apron a long, long while.

Eventually, I realized I was keeping her from more important work and felt ashamed of myself for detaining her. I detached from her embrace and waved her away.

"I'll be fine. Thank you kindly."

She crossed herself, blessed me, and was gone.

Soon two aides came to cover George's face and take his body away on a stretcher. I watched them till they were out of sight, wondering how I would ever fill the gaping chasm in my heart.

Before too much longer, I had my answer. As the sun was rising, all of us in the hall heard the first joyful sounds that had issued there in a long time—the mewling of a newborn baby . . . a newborn baby boy.

—

Now mother and son, and all the rest of us, are gathering strength for the trip home to England. For a time, Darcy even put up the madame and her girls, who kept us in high spirits until they had to return to Calais.

"I've been to places like this before," one of them quipped. "Although, I never stayed all night in one."

The morning they left, Marjorie approached me with a secretive smile. Taking my hand, she put a sealed envelope into it.

"I have a sister in England," she said. "She fought on the wrong side during the Revolution and had to flee for her life. Do you think you could somehow find her and give her this?"

I looked down at the envelope. It was addressed to Madam Marie du Monde. I looked back up at Marjorie, who now wore a knowing smile.

"Perhaps you are acquainted?" she asked with an arch of her brow.

I gave her an arched brow back. "Perhaps I am. At any rate, we'll get this letter to her."

She gave me a hug and a kiss on each cheek, then she and her beauties were gone.

I am dying to steam this envelope open and see what there is to see inside. However, I am not going to do it.

I've learned my lesson the hard way. Some things we aren't meant to know.

Epilogue

June 23, 1816

Dear Diary,

I haven't picked you up in a year and thought that I never would again. However, today is too important to miss making a last entry about it.

Little George has his first birthday today, and the Hafsteds are hosting a grand celebration. The entire household staff is scurrying about downstairs, preparing. Mama and all the Bennet girls are coming, plus countless other people.

Meanwhile, I'm in the nursery, watching young George nap and marveling at how much he looks like his father. He got his father's dark hair and eyes, and his blonde mother's pink complexion, but he's still all George to me. It's almost as if George lives through him—perhaps even the son we lost lives through him, as well.

Brigitta is a wonderful mother, especially considering her youth. As we conquered our language difficulties in the early months together, I learned she has led a tragic life . . . orphaned at an early age and living hand to mouth after that. It wasn't until she met George that she had any good fortune.

She was working in a tavern the soldiers frequented. One night when a drunk accosted her, George came to her defense. According to her, he was a total gentleman. She takes full credit for pursuing him. Whatever the case, they eventually became lovers, and she followed him everywhere—even to war and his death.

She is so grateful to have ample food and shelter that she's been quite generous about sharing her son. The Hafsteds adore him and treat him like their own kin. I suppose I play the role of a loving aunt. Whatever my role with him, I feel fortunate to have something of George.

The little man is stirring in his sleep, so I suppose it's time to close this entry. In the event this is my last one, I should tie up loose ends.

I finally found out what was in Marjorie's letter, and I didn't have to steam it open either. When I gave the envelope to Marie, she glanced at the handwriting, turned pale, and opened it with trembling hands. Scanning it quickly, she let out a cry of joy.

"My sister! She's forgiven me. Here, see for yourself."

She handed me the letter and I read the following:

Dear Sister,

For years now, I've longed to see you dead, as dead as you left my heart when you stole my husband.

An old saying tells us "time heals all wounds." I'm not sure I believe that, but I have found some measure of healing lately.

It began when your young friend dropped into my world. She was on her way to find her man, an English soldier, not a conscript in the French army, as she had told me. She needn't have lied. I have no love for the devil, Napoleon.

My girls and I took her under our wings and soon came to admire her spirit. Travelers share their stories with each other, and I was touched by hers . . . burying a first baby, living on the good graces of wealthy benefactors, and now forging a bold path through war-torn Europe to find her man.

Imagine my shock when I learned that you and your husband were her benefactors.

Despite that pleasant news, my feelings toward you didn't soften immediately. It took hearing more stories about your generosity from our young friend. One day, I awoke and no longer felt anger toward you. It was as if an evil spell had finally been lifted.

We are older now. Who knows how much longer we have on this earth? What good is dwelling in the past?

If you can forgive me for wishing you dead, I can forgive you for stealing Gilles. More than that, I hope to see you again soon. I doubt that you wish to visit a bordello, so may I be so bold as to invite myself there?

Till I hear back from you, I am . . .

> *Your loving sister,*
> *Marjorie*

The letter raised more questions for me than it answered, and I pressed Marie for details. This is what she told me . . .

Before the Revolution, the du Mondes were minor nobility in France. Though aristocrats, they were nearly as poor as their peasants, but treated them as well as they could. Contrary to Marie's version of events, she never married in those days and had no children. However, Marjorie did have a husband, a handsome farmer named Gilles.

When the Revolution broke out, the sisters went separate ways. Marie became a royalist, working undercover to restore the king. Marjorie aligned with the revolutionaries, and a bitter feud erupted.

Eventually, it became too dangerous for Marie. The royalists were being picked off rapidly. Hearing that Marie was about to be arrested, Marjorie rushed to warn her and found her in the arms of Gilles.

As if that weren't bad enough, she learned that Marie had recruited Gilles into becoming a royalist, too. An ugly scene ensued, and Marie and Gilles ran off together. Later, Marjorie learned Marie managed to escape to England. Gilles was not as fortunate. He was captured, tortured, and executed.

Marie continued her royalist efforts from England until the king and queen were beheaded. She then went through two marriages (and widowhoods) with rich, older men, amassing a huge fortune along the way. When the general came into her life, she finally found true love, and happily settled down to the life of a wealthy socialite.

Meanwhile, after losing the du Mondes' estate to the Revolution, Marjorie was penniless. Undaunted, she took to the streets, and became a madame. She prospered in the port town of Calais, but she was constantly reminded of her sister across the channel by the comings and goings of all the Englishmen there. She longed to have her revenge one day, although time and meeting me melted her anger.

From there, a flurry of letters went back and forth between the sisters. Finally, they scheduled a visit, which is happening today. When we gather to celebrate George's first birthday, we will also be celebrating a reconciliation. Marie and Marjorie will be meeting for the first time in decades.

I started this entry saying it would be my last, but as I end it, I'm not so sure. Life is endlessly fascinating. So many mysteries remain to unfold.

What will happen between the two du Monde sisters?

What will George grow up to be?

Will I ever find love again?

Will I ever want to?

All these questions must wait for now. A little boy is reaching his arms out to me, his dark eyes shining, his black curls bobbing. I hear the chatter of people arriving downstairs. I smell the sugary scent of cakes coming from the kitchen and the heady aromas of ladies' perfumes and gentlemen's pipe smoke. I look out the leaded window beside me and see that a glorious summer day has lured several walkers to admire the knot gardens.

I wonder if the general has invited any of his young soldiers? And I wonder if they will be wearing His Majesty's pinks?

THE END

Afterword

ALTHOUGH THIS IS A WORK OF FICTION, MOST OF THE HISTORY in it is based on actual accounts. The details of the Battle of Waterloo, in particular, are drawn from recorded memories of people who fought there, including Arthur Wellesley, the Duke of Wellington, and Napoleon's equerry, Jardin Aine.

England's Prussian allies were indeed instrumental to Wellington defeating Bonaparte. Though they were driven back by him in the days before the battle, they rallied at Waterloo and fought valiantly to vanquish the French there.

The Church and Convent of the Recollets in Nivelles, Belgium, was indeed one of the many places where the wounded from the battle were treated. In addition, Napoleon did spend time in the village of Charleroi in the days before the battle.

What is total fiction is the region of Wexhamshire, England. It does not exist, therefore cannot have a viscount and viscountess. However, it is patterned after many actual such shires which dot the rural countryside all across England.

Similarly, Pemberley, from Jane Austen's original novel, is fictitious. However, Austen historians believe that she modeled it on the palatial manor, Chatsworth, in Derbyshire, while writing *Pride and Prejudice* in the nearby village of Bakewell.

As for the rest of the characters and events in this story, for a writer, even fictitious people and happenings take on a life of their own. That is the case for me with this work. Lydia, Clarice, both of the madams, and all the others live on in my heart, and always will.

Glossary of Terms

Battle of Waterloo   A series of battles ending the Napoleonic Wars, culminating in the final confrontation at Waterloo in present-day Belgium. The Battle of Waterloo is reputed to have had the most casualties of any battle to that time, ushering in the modern era of warfare.

Duke of Wellington   Field Marshal Arthur Wellesley (May 1, 1769 to September 14, 1852), a British soldier and statesman who was a major military and political figure in 19th-century Britain. He is perhaps best known for defeating Napoleon at Waterloo.

Elope   In the parlance of 19th-century Britain, elope simply meant "to run away," not inferring any intention to marry, as is true nowadays. This is significant because when George Wickham and Lydia Bennet are described as having eloped in *Pride and Prejudice*, it does not mean he had any plans to marry her. In addition, if Darcy hadn't intervened on her behalf, he probably never would have, thus ruining her reputation and dishonoring her family.

Equerry   An officer of honor, historically an attendant responsible for the care of an important person's horse(s). The accounts of the Battle of Waterloo in this book are drawn in part from the journals of Napoleon's equerry.

Guy Fawkes Day   Also known as Bonfire Night, one of Britain's most important state holidays, honors the thwarting of a plot by Catholic conspirators to blow up Parliament while Protestant King James I was presiding there. The day is celebrated every November 5 by setting off fireworks, lighting huge bonfires, and burning effigies of Guy Fawkes, the leader of the conspirators, who was captured and executed.

Longbourn   The fictional ancestral home of the Bennet family, in which *Pride and Prejudice* is set

Madam and madame   The two words are sometimes used interchangeably, but more often have specific, different meanings. "Madam" is a polite title used to address a mature woman, often in a somewhat formal context, such as in a business dealing or social interaction. The term "madame" is usually used specifically to describe a prostitute. Both terms are used in different contexts in this story. Marie du Monde is a wealthy socialite, who goes by the title *Madam* du Monde. Her sister, Marjorie du Monde, is a prosperous prostitute, who goes by the title *Madame* du Monde.

Napoleonic Wars   A prolonged series of conflicts over the dominance of Eastern Europe, occurring from 1803 to 1815. Napoleon I led the French, and England led various allied coalitions.

Peignoir   A gauzy, long dressing gown, commonly worn in the bedroom, but also suitable for wear at intimate, evening social gatherings

Peninsular War   A prolonged conflict (May 2, 1808, to April 17, 1814) between Napoleon and the allied forces of Britain, Portugal, and Spain, for control of the Iberian Peninsula. Napoleon lost and was subsequently exiled to the

Italian island of Elba, in an effort to contain him. He later escaped and resumed his efforts to conquer Europe, until he was finally defeated at Waterloo.

Prussia and Prussian   Prussia was the state later known as Germany, and Prussians, the people who inhabited it.

Pinks or His Majesty's Pinks   The crimson tunic worn by English army officers during much of the 1800s

Recollets (also Recollects)   A medieval order of Franciscan friars and nuns, largely missionaries to the poor and in decline by the 1800s

Smelling salts   A mixture of ammonia crystals and/or pungent aromatic herbs kept in a small vial and used since ancient times as a restorative for faintness, largely by genteel women

United Kingdom of the Netherlands   Modern-day Belgium, Holland, and Luxembourg

Acknowledgements

I AM DEEPLY GRATEFUL, ONCE AGAIN, TO MY EDITOR AND friend, Susan E. Lindsey of Savvy Communication, LLC, for both her technical proficiency and creative guidance. This is our fourth writing project, and each time we work together, I have deeper respect and appreciation for her vast imagination, talent, and skill.

I am thankful, too, for another friend, David Williams, author, editor, and curator of the Williams-Nichols Collection at University of Louisville for his proofreading and feedback.

Finally, I thank my friends, Mandy Dick and Monica Schamel, for serving as beta readers for this project. Their encouraging comments, questions, and suggestions were very helpful to me.

About the Author

FRED SCHLOEMER, ED.D., IS A CAREER PSYCHOTHERAPIST, educator, and award-winning author based in Louisville, Kentuky. His book *Parenting Adult Children: Real Stories of Families Turning Challenges into Successes,* won a 2012 Nautilus Book Awards Silver Certificate, for books that promote positive social change. His first novel, *Behind the Footlights,* a tribute to community theater, was named one of *LEO* magazine's "Must Read Books by Kentucky Authors" in 2015. His latest book, *Where the River Birches Beckon,* is a gothic romance about the Underground Railroad in Louisville during the buildup to the Civil War.

He now lives in semi-retirement with his husband, Ernie Schnell, an oncology nurse, on their small horse farm in southern Indiana. Chasing grandchildren, gardening, and writing are his chief occupations nowadays.

He invites readers to contact him at fredschloemer63@gmail .com.

www.ingramcontent.com/pod-product-compliance
Lightning Source LLC
Chambersburg PA
CBHW052136170626
46812CB00004B/1451